**"I'll leave if you w**

"I don't want you to
hands on her shoulders spread, soothing
anxiety and replacing it with something much
nicer.

Lifting both hands, Anna rested them lightly on his
chest. Ah, that felt so good—wear-softened cotton
plaid over solid muscle. She focused on the steady
movement beneath her palms as he breathed.

Gradually his breathing changed and his grip on
her shoulders tightened. He swallowed. "Anna."

She raised her head and met his gaze.

"Do you want me to kiss you?"

"Yes."

Heat flared in his blue-green eyes. "Are you sure?"

"Yes."

Slowly he lowered his head, giving her plenty of
time to change her mind.

She wasn't about to. He wouldn't take it too far. He
wasn't the type to throw caution to the winds.

Maybe this would be their one and only kiss. But it
was one they both wanted, both needed.

# STAND-UP COWBOY

*THE BUCKSKIN BROTHERHOOD*

## Vicki Lewis Thompson

Ocean Dance Press

STAND-UP COWBOY
© 2021 Vicki Lewis Thompson

ISBN: 978-1-946759-99-3

Ocean Dance Press LLC
PO Box 69901
Oro Valley, AZ 85737

Visit the author's website at
VickiLewisThompson.com

# 1

A couple of sacks of groceries tucked behind the seat of his truck, Garrett Whittaker turned off the two-lane onto the Buckskin Ranch road as the sun dipped behind the mountains. Thigh-high snowdrifts on either side testified to the major effort he and his brothers had put forth to clear the road after last night's storm.

*His brothers.* He still marveled at that. He had no biological brothers, or sisters, either, for that matter. But two months ago, right before Christmas, he'd been initiated into the Buckskin Brotherhood, a tight group made up of the wranglers employed on the ranch.

The members of the Brotherhood had worked together for more than ten years, while he'd been on board a mere ten months. Yet they'd invited him in, and the gesture meant more than they could know.

For years he'd wandered, working at different ranches, searching for something he couldn't put into words. Not until he'd found it. Home. For the first time in his life he belonged. He—*what the hell?*

A white car appeared in his rearview mirror, closing fast. Too fast. An older model Taurus that looked vaguely familiar... where had he seen it before?

Whoever it was needed to slow the heck down. The sharp curve had a shady spot where ice collected. Perfect setup for a rollover. He began a weaving pattern in front of them, blocking any attempt to pass.

The driver laid on the horn. Muttering a swear word, he glanced in the rearview mirror. A woman was at the wheel. Good Lord, what was she—

She swerved right and plowed into a snowbank.

The sickening thud echoed in his ears as he slammed to a stop, yanked the emergency brake and leaped out of his truck. He hit the ground running.

She was slumped over the wheel, the white hood of her parka covering her hair. No sign of a deflating airbag. *Dear God.* His insides twisted as a child's wails from a car seat in the back penetrated the closed windows.

Gasping for breath, Garrett grabbed the door handle. Locked. He pounded on the window. "Hey! Are you—"

She moved. Lifted her head.

He exhaled in relief as the window rolled down.

She gazed up at him, her brown eyes wide, her face white as the snow she'd rammed into. "I'm okay."

"Airbag?"

"No airbag. Disabled."

"Why were you speeding?"

"Brakes failed."

"Damn." He reached for the door handle again. Still locked. "Let's get you out of there."

She blinked. "The snowbank?"

"Out of the car. Your kid, too. We'll pull your car out later. You just need to—"

"Right. Turn off the engine." She twisted the key in the ignition and fumbled with her seatbelt. She was shaking.

He leaned down, softened his voice. "Need help?"

"No. But Georgie... he's scared. Could you..."

"Sure." *Georgie.* No wonder the car looked familiar. She was Anna Warren, who'd hired on a couple of months ago to work the reception desk at the raptor sanctuary. She and her son lived in one of the Buckskin's guest cabins. The Taurus was usually parked in front of it.

He kept his tone gentle. She was quivering like a leaf. "You need to unlock the—"

"Oh. Sorry." The locks clicked.

He straightened, headed for the back door and opened it. "Hey, Georgie."

Georgie took one look at him and yelled bloody murder. Not surprising. Word had it that the little boy wasn't fond of men.

The rear-facing car seat was on the passenger side. Sliding onto the worn upholstery, Garrett nudged back his hat and gave the screaming little boy his best smile. "Want a ride in a big truck?"

"Noooo." Georgie twisted as far toward the window as the restraining straps would let him.

"I have cookies."

"Oh, Georgie, c-cookies!" Anna climbed out of the car. "Y-you *love* cookies."

"Mama!" Georgie swiveled in the other direction as he struggled to see her. "Out, Mama!"

"Let him help you, sweetheart. M-mama's a little shaky. B-be a g-good boy for Mama."

Brown eyes exactly the color of Anna's focused a frightened gaze on him.

"Do you like chocolate chip cookies?"

He sucked in a breath and nodded.

"Excellent. Let's get some." Garrett unlatched the restraints quickly before Georgie returned to wailing mode. "Chocolate chips are yummy."

Georgie didn't respond.

"Best cookies ever." He pulled up the hood on Georgie's dark blue snowsuit and lifted the kid free. Tightening his grip on the slippery material, he worked his way out of the back seat.

The little boy let out a whimper. "Don't drop Georgie."

"I promise I won't." Holding him close with one arm, he put a hand on the snowsuit hood to make sure the boy's head cleared the opening. Then he planted his boots in the slush, tucked Georgie against his chest and stood.

"Thank you."

He turned as Anna came toward him, her purse strap looped across her chest, bandolier-style. Her cheeks had gained some color and she wasn't shaking much.

She held out her arms. "I can take him, now."

"Are you sure? Because I can—"

"Mama!" Georgie lunged for her, ending the discussion.

"I'm here, sweetie." She gathered him close. "I'm here, baby boy." Bowing her head, she gave him a kiss on the cheek. "Sorry I scared you."

He clung to her and buried his face against her neck. "Wanna go home."

"We will." Her gaze lifted to connect with Garrett's. "The pedal went to the floor. I didn't know what to do."

"You did fine. Are you sure you're okay? Did you hit your head? Does your neck hurt? Or—"

"Nothing hurts. I braced for the impact. It was the adrenaline rush that sidelined me. It's fading."

"Then let's get you and Georgie home." He put his arm around her shoulders to guide her toward the truck. "I wasn't bluffing about the cookies. I was on my way back from the market."

"Cookies, Mama." Georgie's comment was muffled against her collar.

Thank God he'd bought some. "Coming up, sport."

"Just one," Anna murmured. "Or he'll spoil his dinner."

"Got it." He opened the passenger door and helped her in. She didn't wince or catch her breath during that maneuver, so maybe she'd escaped injury, after all.

"You left the truck motor running."

"Didn't bother to turn it off. I just—"

"Raced to our rescue." Her dark eyes warmed with gratitude.

"I was so afraid that you... anyway, your car seat won't fit in my truck, but I can belt you in together and drive super slow."

"No worries. We were in worse shape in a car with no brakes."

"But you made it." He grabbed the seat belt buckle, reached around both passengers and clicked it in place. "I'll get his cookie." He closed the door and jogged around to the driver's side.

He'd bagged the groceries himself and made sure the cookies were on top so they wouldn't be crushed. Reaching behind the seat, he picked up the package, tore it open and pulled out two cookies. He handed the first one up to the front seat. "For Georgie."

He reached for it. "Cookie." His voice was a hoarse croak. The little guy had been terrified, too, first by the crash and then by a stranger hauling him out of the car.

"And one for you." He held out the second cookie to Anna.

"Oh, I don't need—"

"Yes, you do. That was a rough experience. Take the cookie."

"Okay, I will." She accepted it and graced him with a tiny smile. "Thanks."

"You're welcome." Closing the package of cookies, he swung into the driver's seat and shut the door.

She chewed and swallowed a bite of cookie. "These are delicious. I've never bought cookies at the market."

"I didn't used to. Made my own. These are better than mine." He buckled up, put the truck in gear and pulled out slowly.

"Better than mine, too. You bake?"

"On occasion. I'm more into meal preparation, though."

"Then you must be Garrett."

"Yes, ma'am."

"I'm still getting acquainted with everyone. I'm glad to meet you, although the circumstances leave something to be desired. You can't imagine how much this—"

"My pleasure, Anna."

"I've heard you're the newest member of the Brotherhood."

"From Jake?"

"Good guess. He's provided the deets on everybody. He's a lot more entertaining than the last boss I had."

"Jake's more entertaining than most people on the planet. How do you like working the reception desk at Raptors Rise?"

"Love it. Jake's giving me a crash course in birds of prey. Honestly, if I didn't need the money, I'd do the job for free." She broke off a section of cookie and popped it into her mouth.

"Jake says you're perfect for it. He and Leo came up with the idea of hiring you after we watched the Operation Santa video on Christmas Day."

"Oh."

Had he embarrassed her by mentioning she'd been a recipient of the charity? A quick glance confirmed that she was blushing. "Listen, I think it's awesome that you signed Georgie up for a visit from Santa."

"Don't want Santa," Georgie muttered before taking another bite of his cookie.

Her blush deepened. "I never should have insisted on having him sit on Leo's lap. I was so busy taking pictures I didn't notice he kicked him in the crotch."

"No permanent damage done and it makes a great story."

"If you say so." She let out another sigh. "I suppose this brake incident will make a great story someday, but I'm not feeling it right now."

"Wouldn't expect you to. What's the deal with the disabled airbag?"

"The previous owner was a small person and was afraid of it. I'm not all that big, either. Knowing an airbag wouldn't hit me in the face and chest made it easier to run into the snowbank."

"I suppose it would. And you had the presence of mind to brace yourself." He took the road at a snail's pace. "Would you have passed me if I'd let you by?"

"Probably, but I'm glad you didn't. I was picking up speed, trying to picture the curve ahead, knowing it might be icy and getting more frantic by the second."

"Me, too. I thought you were crazy."

"Which I was when my foot went straight to the floor."

"That's a horrible sensation."

"It's happened to you?"

"Once. I should have noticed the fluid was leaking, but it was roundup at the outfit I worked for and I wasn't paying close attention to my vehicle."

"Should I have known?"

"Not necessarily. It could've been a slow leak that suddenly got worse."

"I try to watch for things like that. I taught myself how to change the oil. I haven't had to take it to a mechanic since I moved here." She sighed. "Guess that streak's over."

"I could replace the brake lines for you."

"Oh, no, I couldn't ask—"

"You didn't. I offered. That kind of thing is fun for me and I have the tools. Almost became a mechanic, but I like horses better."

"Well..." She took a deep breath. "Thank you. That's very kind. I can at least pay for the parts."

"All right." Clearly that would ease her discomfort about accepting his help. The parts wouldn't cost much compared to what a garage would charge for labor.

"I hate to ask, considering your generosity, but how soon do you think—"

"I'll see if Jake can help me tow it back here tomorrow and I'll pick up the parts in town on my lunch break. I'm off tomorrow afternoon. If everything goes smoothly, I could have it back to you tomorrow night. Partly depends on how the front end is."

"Oh." She'd just taken another bite. She finished chewing it and swallowed. "I completely spaced that possibility. The front end could be knocked out of alignment. The headlights could be broken. The radiator could be—"

"We just plowed the road this morning, so the snow might be loose enough that nothing is damaged." Or the front end of her car could be a disaster, but imagining the worst wouldn't help.

"Fingers crossed. I need that car to get groceries and take Georgie to daycare. In fact, I need to figure out how to get him there in the morning."

"You could borrow my truck."

"No way. I've never driven one. I don't suppose there's a car rental in town? I've never heard of one but maybe—"

"Not in Apple Grove. You'd have to go to Great Falls."

"Impractical. Maybe that old cab driver Alfred—"

"I wouldn't trust Alfred's vehicle not to break down along the way. We'll work something out. Henri has a four-door truck. She could accommodate Georgie's car seat."

"I hate to bother her, though. I'd have to go with her or Georgie would panic, so she couldn't even combine it with a shopping trip. She'd have to come right back. I open the visitor center at nine."

"Jake would cover for you."

"That would throw his schedule off. I—"

"Anna, stuff happens. And the Buckskin gang is a flexible bunch, eager to help anyone, especially one of our own."

She gazed at him. "That's nice to hear."

"I'm serious. We roll with the punches."

"I've noticed. But I've never thought of myself as one of you."

"You haven't?" He glanced at her in surprise. "Did Henri forget to give you her *Welcome to the Buckskin* speech? I got it, and I assumed she went through that spiel with everyone she hired."

"She did give me that speech. And everyone's been lovely. But since I have Georgie, I can't go to the Choosy Moose and party with you guys, so I don't really feel—"

"Henri said she's offered to watch Georgie so you could have a night out now and then."

"She did, but I don't want to impose."

He smiled. "Trust me, it wouldn't be an imposition. Have you noticed how she dotes on Cleo Marie?"

"That's different. She thinks of CJ and all of you as her sons. She considers that baby her granddaughter."

"She'd be thrilled to shower the same kind of attention on Georgie. That woman's heart is as big as Montana."

"I believe you. I'll think about it." She glanced at him for a moment before returning her gaze to the view out the windshield. "The thing is, I'm not used to asking for help. When I left my ex, I was determined to make it on my own. And I did, until I lost my job."

"Leo saw that determination when he met you. That's why he wanted to help you find work that paid enough to support you and Georgie."

"That was the first time I asked for charity. I debated and debated and finally went for it, mostly because I was hoping he'd have fun. He was excited, but all he'd seen was the cartoon version of Santa, so he didn't understand..." Her voice trailed off and she glanced down at Georgie, who was munching away on his cookie. "Wow, son, you're getting crumbs all over."

"Crumbs, Mama." Georgie surveyed the array scattered around him.

"Don't worry about it, Anna. I don't care."

"I do." She started plucking bits of cookie from the leather seat and shoving them in her pocket. "This is a very nice truck. Did you restore it?"

"I did. But I'm not worried about cookie crumbs."

"And if you were, I'll bet you wouldn't say so. You've been awesome through this whole episode. I don't know what your dinner plans are, but—"

"Just fixing something for myself at the bunkhouse. I'm batching it there for now. Leo spends most of his free time with Fiona."

"Then let me cook dinner for you. It's the least I can do."

It was on the tip of his tongue to offer to cook for her, instead. Preparing food for others was another one of his favorite things, and since the members of the Brotherhood only gathered at the bunkhouse once a month, he didn't get that pleasure as often. He had several dinner options in the shopping bags.

But clearly she was looking for a way to thank him for helping her through a crisis. A wise man would shut up and let her do that. He hadn't always been wise, but now that he lived on the Buckskin Ranch, he was gaining wisdom every day.

He glanced over at her. "I'm grateful for the invitation. It's not much fun eating alone."

# 2

Anna finished off her cookie and began cleaning up the crumbs Georgie had dropped. Feeding Garrett was the decent and obvious gesture to make, if it didn't backfire on her.

It wasn't a date. She'd vowed not to date until Georgie was older — *much* older. She also hadn't cooked for anyone other than Georgie in more than a year. And Georgie likely wouldn't react well to having Garrett in the house.

As he parked in front of the guest cabin Henri had offered as part of her salary, she began to fret about whether she'd tidied up enough. The interior of his truck had been spotless before Georgie had scattered crumbs everywhere.

Maybe she could buy some time. "You can just drop me off." She looked over at him. "You probably want to take your groceries to the bunkhouse."

"Don't need to. In this weather, they'll be fine in the truck." He switched off the engine. "I'll come around and help you out."

"Thank you." So much for making a quick sweep of the house and wiping off sticky surfaces. She unbuckled the seatbelt. "We're home, Georgie."

"Where's the man?"

"His name is Garrett."

Georgie stood on her lap, peered out the windshield and pointed. "There! Grit's coming, Mama."

"To help us out."

"No."

"It's fine, Georgie. He's eating with us tonight."

"In my house?"

"In *our* house." Georgie had recently started identifying what was his and he'd claimed the entire guest cabin.

"Don't *want* Grit in my house."

"He's a very nice—" The passenger door opened.

"I can take him." Garrett reached for Georgie.

"*No, no Grit!*" He drew back.

She snugged him against her hip. "That's okay. I've got him." She started to reach for the handle on the truck's doorframe.

"I'll help you down."

She glanced at him standing in the glow of the cab's dome light with his hand outstretched. Her heart did a fast two-step. His eyes were light green, almost blue.

And the way he was looking at her filled her chest with warmth and longing. That hadn't happened in a very long time. She put her hand in his strong grip and stepped on the running board.

"Mama, no! No Grit!" Georgie began to struggle.

"He's not going to take you, son." She tightened her hold and Garrett steadied her as she climbed down. "Sorry about that," she murmured.

"Don't want Grit," Georgie muttered loud enough for Garrett to hear.

"Would it be better if I didn't stay?"

She met his gaze. A tropical sea. She'd never seen one except in pictures, but his eyes were exactly that color. "I'd like you to stay if you're willing. I don't want certain people to think they're in charge."

He flashed her a quick smile. "Understood. Did he just call me Grit?"

"'Fraid so."

"No worries. I kind of like it."

"Give me a moment with him, please."

"Absolutely."

She carried Georgie to the porch, sat on one of the Adirondack chairs and settled him on her lap. "Georgie, look at me."

He made eye contact with obvious reluctance. "Don't want Grit, Mama."

"I know. But he's staying for dinner. He's our guest."

His expression grew stormy.

"He rescued us. Like we rescued the bird at the other house. Remember?"

He nodded. "He was stuck."

"We took off the string around his leg. We rescued him."

"He flyed away."

"Yes, but I'm sure he was grateful."

"But he flyed *away*." He turned toward Garrett. His logic was flawed but his implication was clear. Time for their rescuer to fly away. The sooner, the better.

"Garrett is staying for dinner. I want you to be nice to him and mind your manners."

He sighed and nodded.

"You could show him your moose."

"No."

"No, *ma'am.*"

His *no, ma'am* was barely audible, but she'd take it. "Okay, then. Let's go inside." Setting him on his feet, she stood and fished her keys out of her purse. "Thanks for waiting!" she called out to Garrett. "Come on in. We'll make a fire and have s'mores for dessert."

Georgie gasped with delight. "'mores?"

"If you're a good boy." Bribing him with food was setting a bad precedent, but if it got her through the evening, she'd do a course correction in the morning. She unlocked the door.

The minute she opened it, Georgie rushed inside. "*My* house." He started to close the door.

She put a hand on it. "Georgie."

His voice dropped to a whisper. "My house." Then he dashed away.

"I love s'mores." Garrett climbed the porch steps and followed her into the house. "Haven't had them in a while, either."

"They're one of Georgie's favorites." She flicked the switch by the door that turned on a lamp in the living room.

Her son had disappeared, but the light was on in his bedroom, revealing his whereabouts. She'd put a stool next to the wall and using it to reach the switch thrilled him.

She glanced around. His wooden train set lay in disarray in front of the fireplace and the worn blanket he'd used to make a tent was draped over the couch, but otherwise the room was in decent shape.

When she turned on the light hanging over the round kitchen table, his cereal bowl sat there. She'd run out of time to supervise having him carry it to the sink.

"This is nice," Garrett said. "I haven't been in one of Henri's new two-bedroom cabins."

"It's a luxury for me. The little house I was renting was a one-bedroom. Georgie loves having his own space." She removed her jacket and hung it on the coat tree by the door. "Can I take your—"

"Thanks. I've got it." He shrugged out of his shearling jacket and settled it on a hook. His hat joined it. "This is probably one of Henri's antique finds."

"I thought it looked old."

"She haunts the antique shops searching for coat trees."

The sound of a childish voice carrying on a conversation drifted from Georgie's bedroom.

Garrett glanced at her. "Is he on the phone?"

"He's talking to his moose."

"The one he got from Operation Santa?"

"Yep. He liked the other toys, but he adores that little plush moose. He named it after his bestie at daycare. When he's upset, he tells his troubles to Carl."

"Leo will be glad to hear the moose is a hit."

"I keep meaning to tell him, and apologize about Georgie kicking him, but our paths don't cross. I see Jake and Millie all the time, but everybody else, not so much."

"Does Georgie get along with Jake?"

"Not really. He's not good with men in general, and it didn't help that he spent the past year almost exclusively with me." She paused. A good hostess would offer a beverage at this point. She was so out of practice. "Would you like something to drink?"

"Only if you'll join me."

"Sure. I have some cider in the fridge."

"Perfect."

She headed for the kitchen nook and turned on the oven to preheat it. Then she opened the refrigerator and pulled out a package of chicken breasts. "I was planning on having these for dinner." She usually baked several at once so she'd have leftovers. But she'd happily forego leftovers to provide Garrett with a hearty meal.

"Sounds great. Can I help?"

She hesitated. This was getting cozier by the minute but his friendly offer appealed to her. "That would be nice." She handed him a bottle of cider and an opener.

"Don't need that, thanks." He twisted off the cap.

"Doesn't that hurt?" She popped the cap off a second bottle.

"I'm used to it. Tough hands."

Strong hands. Callused? Maybe, but his warm grip had stirred a yearning she'd be wise to squelch.

He tipped his bottle in her direction. "Here's to surviving a ruptured brake line."

"With your help." She tapped her bottle to his and took a sip. "If you hadn't forced me to run into the snowbank..."

"All's well that ends well." He took a swallow of his cider. "But let's not do that again, okay?"

She smiled. "Okay. Were you scared?"

"I was. Bad enough when I thought you were some crazy stranger, but when you mentioned Georgie and I realized you were one of us..." He took a deep breath. "Not good."

"That's sweet, since you don't really know me."

"Technically I don't, but Jake brags on you quite a bit. And Henri's told me she's impressed with how you're raising Georgie."

She made a face. "If she'd seen his performance tonight, she might not be so impressed."

"Has he always disliked men?"

She hesitated. Not her favorite topic.

"Hey, if that was too personal, you don't have to—"

"The answer is yes, he has. Brad, my ex, was extremely jealous of the attention I gave Georgie. I hadn't seen that coming. After ten months of living in hell, I'd squirreled away enough to leave."

Compassion warmed his gaze. "Sounds grim."

"It was harder on Georgie than me. In that time, he learned that men are scary people who yell, slam doors and break dishes."

"Does Georgie see him now?"

"No, thank goodness. He took a job selling real estate in Texas."

"Child support?"

She shook her head. "I was thrilled to be rid of him. Tracking him down and forcing him to pay would be a nasty business."

"Seems wrong that he can abandon his responsibility, though."

"It is wrong, but I've made peace with that in exchange for never having to see him again. I would have been fine if the insurance agent I worked for hadn't decided to retire early and move to Florida."

"But hey, you ended up with a more interesting job."

"That's for sure." She gestured around the cabin. "And a fabulous place to live, with new appliances instead of the dicey ones in the house I'd rented. Speaking of appliances, the oven's preheated so I'd better get the chicken ready."

"Put me to work."

"You can fix the potatoes. I usually make country fries but you're welcome to do something else with them if you want."

"Country fries are my favorite. I like browning them in a skillet and then baking them, if that works for you."

"That's how I do it." Any anxiety she'd had about feeding this man evaporated. He was easy. The evening might turn out to be fun, after all. For her, anyway. Georgie wasn't happy about the situation, but she'd stand firm on her decision to host Garrett in *their* house.

# 3

"Ever eaten with a two-year-old?"

"Can't say I have." Garrett finished browning the potatoes, transferred them to a baking dish and added a few spices from a drawer next to the stove.

Sharing dinner preparation with Anna was easy. They worked at a similar speed and hadn't bumped into each other once. Cooking alongside Jake was smooth like that.

Meal prep with Anna had the added buzz of a slow-burn mutual attraction. Jake's and Henri's praise had made him eager to meet her. Now that he had, her smile and the sparkle in her dark eyes teased him with possibilities.

"I should stop calling Georgie a two-year-old." She brought out ingredients for a tossed salad and a baguette for the garlic toast she wanted to add to the meal. "He'll be three in April, so he's not nearly as messy with his food."

"Not messy, Mama!"

Garrett turned as Georgie tore out of the kitchen nook and back into his room. "Did you know he was spying on us?"

"I saw him. I decided to pretend he wasn't there and give him a compliment."

"I hate that he's spooked by me."

"It's not personal. It wouldn't matter what man was standing in the kitchen." She handed him the baguette, a breadboard and a knife.

He started slicing. "Seems like it would be good to have him spend time with men who don't yell and throw things." Or one man, namely him.

"Carl's mom suggested that, to desensitize him. but I'm not sure how to go about it." She set the table for three. One chair had a booster seat and she put smaller utensils at that place. "I'm not hauling him to work with me so he can get used to Jake. That would be unprofessional. And I can't ask some guy to come hang out in the evening so I can reprogram my son."

"Why not? I'd do it."

She stared at him. "That makes no sense. You have a life, things to do. For all I know you're dating someone and—"

"Not at the moment. Leo and I are the only two wranglers in the bunkhouse and he's hardly ever there at night. I could spend some time over here. I don't yell and break dishes."

"I'm sure you don't, but—"

"It might not take all that long. A few quiet evenings might be enough to show him all men aren't scary."

"I think that's overly optimistic, but since it sounds like you have some free time...."

"And I'm really not a fan of eating alone."

"I'll admit it's an interesting idea." Her tone was businesslike, matter-of-fact. She almost hid the flash of awareness in her eyes by glancing away.

"Then let's do it. His mistrust of men isn't a huge problem now, but what happens if his first-grade teacher is a guy?"

"I've thought of that scenario. Even if it's not his first-grade teacher, it'll be someone down the line. His pediatrician is a woman but she could move. It'll become an issue eventually."

"Let me help, Anna." Yeah, he had an ulterior motive, but he also wanted to help her kid.

"Just to be clear, our time together wouldn't be a date."

"Right." So much for his ulterior motive. If she felt the need to emphasize that fact, he'd honor her wishes.

"I'm not dating anyone until Georgie's... I don't know. Maybe in college? I made him suffer for one bad choice. I won't risk putting him through anything like that again."

"I understand." Georgie wasn't the only person who'd been traumatized by that dude. She was gun-shy and he didn't blame her. Those ten months must have been even worse than she'd let on.

"We're almost ready to eat. I'll go find out if Georgie will be joining us tonight."

"I don't know how he could resist the aroma of that chicken." He glanced toward Georgie's bedroom as she headed in that direction. If the little guy had crept out to watch them fix dinner, that was a positive sign. He might be scared, but he was curious, too.

"Time to wash your hands for dinner, Georgie," she called out.

A little face peeked around the doorframe and popped back inside. Anna walked into the room and the two of them talked in low tones. She was in there quite a while.

She came out alone. "He wants you to leave, but I've told him you're not going to."

"Is he hungry?"

"Yes, so I have a couple of options. I can tell him no dinner unless he comes out and eats with us. Or I can offer to take him his food if he agrees to leave the door open."

"I don't think forcing him to be with me is a good way to go."

She gazed at him. "You're right. It's not. The disciplinarian in me wanted to take that first route, but if he leaves the door open he can hear us and get used to you being in the house."

"And he can spy on us if he wants to."

She smiled. "Which he probably will. I'll go see if he'll take that deal." Moments later she was back. "He went for it."

"Good."

"I'll get his tray ready. Would you be willing to start a fire? He reminded me about s'mores, and that might be what finally brings him out."

"I'm on it." He crossed to the living area and moved the wooden train, a set much like the one he'd longed for as a kid. Georgie had drawn the crummy dad card, but his awesome mother made up for it.

By the time he had a fire crackling on the grate, she'd returned from taking Georgie his meal.

"He heard you making a fire."

Placing the folding screen in front of it, he stood. "Let me guess. He doesn't want Grit to stay for s'mores."

"He doesn't, but I told him I promised you could have some, and I keep my promises."

"So do I." He held her gaze for a moment, enjoying the tell-tale flicker of emotion in her eyes. "Ready to eat?"

"I'm starving. Evidently crashing my car into a snowbank gave me an appetite. Is it okay if we just dish ourselves from the pans?"

"As opposed to what?" He followed her over to the kitchen nook.

"Oh, you know. Putting the potatoes in a nice bowl and arranging the chicken on a platter that we bring to the table." She took two plates out of the cupboard and handed him one.

"Just dirties up more dishes."

She laughed. "I like how you think." She helped herself to a scoop of potatoes, a piece of chicken, a generous amount of salad and two pieces of garlic toast. "My mother would have a fit if she knew I'd asked you to load up from the kitchen counter. Guests are supposed to be served from dishes brought to the table."

"Then she'd better not visit the Buckskin bunkhouse. We hardly ever do it that way." He followed her lead and took the same amount of food she had.

"That bunkhouse sounds like a fun place to live."

"It has been. It still is when the Brotherhood gets together once a month."

"Jake told me you do a sleepover."

"We do. We're debating whether this month it should be before or after Valentine's Day." He pulled out her chair.

She flashed him a smile. "Thanks." Then she glanced at his plate as he took the seat across from her. "That's all you're eating?"

"It's plenty."

"It's plenty for me, but I can't believe it's enough for you. You're twice my size."

"That doesn't mean I have to eat like a horse."

"Garrett, tell the truth. Normally you'd take two pieces of chicken and larger servings of potatoes and salad."

He was amused by her tone. She probably spoke to Georgie like that when he wasn't being straight with her. "Well…"

"Go get more food."

"Okay." He pushed back his chair. "But if we're going to share dinner more often, let me bring in some groceries."

"Are you kidding? You're doing me a huge favor. The least I can do is feed you."

"All right, then. Thank you. It's a treat to have someone else plan the meals for a change."

"What are some of your favorites?"

"Oh, hey, I don't want you to start making things you wouldn't usually—"

"Is there anything you dislike?"

"No, ma'am." He returned to the table with a more robust serving of food. "I'll eat anything that's put in front of me."

"Spoken like a kid who was told to clean his plate." She picked up a fork and took a bite of the potatoes. "Mm."

He smiled. Pleasing someone with his cooking was always a goal, but tonight he was especially happy that she liked the way he'd fixed the potatoes. He let the comment about cleaning his plate go by. No reason to dive into his unappetizing childhood.

She cut into her chicken. "What does Valentine's Day have to do with when you schedule your Brotherhood overnight?"

"If we have it a few days before, we can gather suggestions about how to make the occasion special for our lady. If we gather sometime afterward, we can find out how everyone's plans worked out."

"You talk about such things?"

"In general terms, sure. Not the intimate details, but if somebody is having an issue with the woman in his life, he's likely to ask for advice or even want assistance. I got my first taste of it last spring when Jake was on the outs with Millie."

"Whatever you guys suggested must've worked since they got married on New Year's Eve."

"Oh, it worked." He chuckled. "It was an epic stunt. He dressed up like the Lone Ranger and jumped through flaming hoops on a white horse. We rode along as his posse."

"What in the world prompted *that*?"

"Millie accused him of acting like the Lone Ranger instead of treating her like a partner. She said he'd have to jump through flaming hoops before she'd take him back. I'll never forget the look on her face when he literally did that. She was stunned."

Anna grinned. "Gee, I wonder why. Does Valentine's Day involve epic stunts, too?"

"I have no idea. I wasn't here for Valentine's Day last year."

"If that was your first taste of Brotherhood interventions, there must be more stories."

"Jake hasn't told you any?"

"Not really. He just gave me some key points on each of you. He didn't breathe a word about dressing up like the Lone Ranger. It adds a whole new dimension to his personality."

"Speaking of Jake, I'd better call him and ask about towing your car out in the morning."

"Oh, right." Some of the sparkle left her dark eyes.

"While I'm doing that, you could contact Henri."

She took a deep breath. "I guess."

"Anna, she'd want you to ask. If she can't do it, she'll figure out who can. Please call her."

"Okay."

# 4

While Garrett retrieved his phone from his jacket, she reluctantly took hers out of her purse. What if her brake line had been leaking and she'd failed to notice a spot under the car? Garrett had tried to let her off the hook, but her car, her responsibility.

And now she had to ask Henri to drive her and Georgie into town in the morning, and possibly make the reverse trip tomorrow afternoon. Her chest tightened as she made the call.

"Hey, Anna!" Henri sounded in good spirits. "What's up?"

"I hope I didn't catch you at a bad time."

"Not at all. Ben and I are having happy hour in front of the fire."

"Oh." She'd interrupted their cozy evening. But what was done was done. She soldiered on. "I have a huge favor to ask. Would you possibly be able to drive me and Georgie to his daycare in the morning? I usually leave around eight-fifteen."

"Sure, I can do that. Happy to. Do you have issues with your car?"

"You could say that. The brakes went out on the way home tonight and I—"

"Oh, my *God*. Are you okay? Is Georgie okay?"

"We're fine, thanks to Garrett. It's a long story and I don't want to keep you on the phone. In order to stop the car, I... had to hit a snowbank."

"Oh, honey. That sounds traumatic. I'm so sorry. But you and Georgie have no ill effects?"

"We don't. And Garrett was in front of me, so he ran to the rescue."

"Of course he did. I'm so glad he was there! How's your car?"

"We don't know yet. It's still in the snowbank. Garrett's calling Jake now to ask for his help in getting it out tomorrow. But that's the other thing. We should probably leave a few minutes early so I can transfer Georgie's car seat from my car to your truck."

"You bet. I need to get savvy about car seats so I'll be ready when I'm allowed to take Cleo Marie in my truck, so this will be good practice. I'll pick you up at eight-ten in the morning. That should get you back in time to open up the visitor center."

"That's perfect. Thank you so much, Henri."

"I'm more than happy to do it. I've been wanting to get better acquainted with your little guy, so this will be fun. See you in the morning and give Garrett a hug for me. Tell him he's my hero for coming to your rescue."

"I'll tell him. He's mine, too." But she wasn't giving him a hug. "Have a nice evening."

"You, too."

Filled with equal measures of gratitude and relief, Anna ended the call. Asking for favors would never be fun for her, but Henri had made it less painful.

She returned to the table, where Garrett stood, his phone still to his ear as he talked with Jake.

His wide grin indicated Jake was likely teasing him about something. "What's wrong with weaving in front of a speeding car? It worked, didn't it?" He laughed. "Well, aside from that. I'll see that it gets fixed." He paused. "Yes, I've done some body work." He rolled his eyes. "You know what I meant."

Turning, he winked at her. "I'll give her your best. Just a sec." He pressed the phone against his chest. "Can Henri take you in the morning?"

"Yes."

"Good." He put the phone to his ear again. "She's all set with Henri for the morning run. We'll see what kind of magic I can work. Maybe she won't need Millie for the afternoon trip, but I'll relay the offer. And tell Millie thanks. Yeah, you, too, bro. G'night."

"He didn't approve of your method of slowing me down?"

"He said I should've gone ahead to the curve and parked over the icy patch so you could swerve around me."

"And then what? I would have taken that curve too fast. Even without the ice, I might have flipped."

He shuddered. "What a nightmare scenario."

"Your method worked fine. Henri said to tell you that you're her hero."

He blushed. "I did what anyone would have."

That pink on his cheeks was adorable. "Except Jake, apparently."

"Jake would have done the weave thing. I'd bet money on it. He just loves giving everyone a hard time." Laying his phone by his plate, he walked around the table and pulled out her chair. "We should finish before everything gets cold. The chicken's delicious, by the way."

"Thank you." She sat and retrieved her napkin from beside her plate. "Millie offered to take me to pick up Georgie tomorrow afternoon?"

"She did." He rounded the table and levered himself into his chair. "I'm hoping I'll have your car back by then. We'll see."

"Will you text me about the front end once you and Jake pull the car out?"

"I will." He lowered his voice and leaned closer. "Can you see Georgie's bedroom door from where you're sitting?"

"Uh-huh."

"I'm pretty sure he popped out to check on us while I was talking to Jake, but then I lost track of him."

She dropped her voice to a murmur. "He's on the couch, peering over the back of it. I'm pretending I don't know he's there. Keep talking. Got any other Jake stories?"

"More than we have time for."

\* \* \*

Anna hadn't shared a meal with a guy in quite a while. She was enjoying herself. Garrett kept her entertained with stories of Jake's antics and she'd never look at her boss the same way again.

They were almost finished eating when Garrett launched into a description of Christmas Eve in the waiting room of the maternity ward at Apple Grove General. Jake had grabbed that opportunity to coax Millie into proposing.

When he described how Jake took one of Santa's knees and Millie took the other, she cracked up. She'd seen Leo wearing the Santa suit on Yule when he'd brought Georgie's presents, so she had no trouble picturing the scene.

"They just managed to get it done when CJ came out to announce Cleo Marie's birth. Quite a night."

"So what about their wedding on New Year's Eve? Did Jake pull anything, then?"

"Believe it or not, he played it straight. Got emotional, in fact. Not a dry eye in the house when those two finally said their vows."

"That's nice. Jake and Millie are great together. I wish them a lifetime of happiness."

"I don't think there's any doubt. They've sorted through their issues and they're solid." He motioned to her empty plate. "Looks like you're done."

"Sure am."

"Ready to move on to s'mores?"

"Absolutely." She glanced toward the couch. "I'd better check on Georgie and find out if he ate all his dinner."

"I did, Mama!"

Garrett turned around just as Georgie's head disappeared behind the back of the couch. "Where'd that voice come from, Anna?" He widened his eyes in mock amazement. "I don't see anybody."

"Must be the invisibility cloak in action."

"Grit can't see Georgie." The soft murmur came from the other side of the couch.

Garrett muffled a laugh with his napkin, making it sound like a cough.

He won points for that. Georgie's fear was real to him and laughing at it wouldn't be kind.

Leaning across the table, Garrett mouthed the words *what now?*

She pushed her plate aside, leaned in, too, and dropped her voice to a murmur. "He's under the blanket that was—"

"Saw it." He was almost close enough to kiss.

She hadn't kissed a man in a long time, hadn't had the urge. She wouldn't be kissing this one, despite his appealing mouth. "We'll take the fixings in and pretend we don't know where he is."

"Do you let him toast the marshmallows?"

"With supervision, but not if he keeps the blanket."

"Good call."

She focused on his eyes instead of his mouth. Not much better. The flicker of interest in his blue-green gaze beckoned her to come closer.

"What about eating s'mores under the blanket? Sounds messy."

"I can wash it." This close encounter was giving her a buzz. And she liked it.

"Guess so." A soft smile curved his sculpted lips. "Then let's see what—"

"No kissing!"

Surprise jerked her backward. She hadn't been thinking about kissing Garrett — not really — but Georgie must have seen things differently.

Shrugging, she flashed Garrett a smile. "Kids." Pushing back her chair, she stood.

"Yeah." He returned her smile and got up, too. "I can load the dishwasher while you organize the stuff for s'mores."

"Good idea. Thanks." She took the chocolate bars and bag of marshmallows out of the cupboard and carried them into the living room.

The dancing flames had subsided, leaving red-hot coals. Perfect for toasting marshmallows. The long-handled forks hung by the fireplace. She'd only bought two. Hadn't ever expected a third person would share this experience.

Her son had tucked himself under the worn plaid blanket and was hiding in a corner of the couch. He lifted an edge of the blanket and peered out at her. "Hi, Mama."

"Hi, Georgie." She laid the supplies on the unoccupied part of the couch. "If you keep that blanket wrapped around you, I can't let you roast marshmallows. It's not safe."

"Why?"

"The blanket could catch on fire."

"It won't. I be careful."

"I'm not taking the chance of you getting that blanket near the flames."

"But—"

"Either you can remain invisible and eat the s'mores I fix for you, or you can come out from under the blanket and I'll help you roast your own marshmallows."

"Mama, I can—"

"That's it, Georgie. Those are your two choices." She fetched the folding table they used, about the size of a TV tray, and set it up in front of the couch. She laid the supplies there.

"Looks like you're ready." Garrett walked in from the kitchen nook and Georgie dived under the blanket. "You and Captain Invisible." He glanced at her. "Any chance our friend will come out to toast marshmallows?"

"I don't know. What do you say Captain Invisible?"

"Don't want Grit."

"Well, Grit, I mean Garrett, is staying for s'mores. Are you coming out?"

"No."

"No, what?"

"No, ma'am."

"Okay, then." She walked over to the wall, took down the forks and handed one to Garrett. "Are you a slow, steady toaster or marshmallow-on-fire person?"

He smiled. "What do you think?"

"Slow, steady toaster."

"Afraid not." He took a marshmallow out of the package and impaled it on his fork. "I like to catch these babies on fire."

"I'm a slow, steady toaster."

"There's room for all kinds." He crouched beside the fire.

The position tightened the denim covering his thighs and backside. Nice. Having him around for several evenings in a row would be an interesting challenge.

But his presence would benefit Georgie tremendously. Nobody had to know how much she was enjoying the view.

# 5

Garrett munched on his graham-cracker sandwich with a charred, squishy marshmallow cuddled up to a square of stubbornly un-melted chocolate in the middle. Tasted great.

And he had a dilemma.

Anna needed him to help her with Georgie and she enjoyed his company. He enjoyed hers, too. Very much. Maybe a little too much considering the circumstances.

On one level, he got it. She'd been burned and wasn't ready to jump back into the fire. He wasn't like her ex—that much was a given—but he was a man. Close enough, unfortunately. She was as spooked, or maybe even more so, than Georgie.

What was he supposed to do? Abandoning the project wasn't an option. He could fix the Georgie problem, no question. All he needed was time.

But that meant time spent with Anna, because she needed to be there, too. Georgie would freak out if she left him alone with big, scary Grit. That meant the three of them were locked in a cozy situation that scared the devil out of her and made him wary, too. He didn't favor getting his heart smashed to bits.

Anna and Georgie had the wherewithal to accomplish that. All he had to do was get attached to mother and son, then have Anna remind him that she wasn't interested in dating.

He should be honest with himself. He wanted to help Georgie get over his mistrust of men because it would be good for the kid.

But he also wanted that outcome because it would be good for the mother, who might then consider getting involved with someone—him— before Georgie enrolled in college. He was a patient man, but his family jewels would dry up and fall off if he had to wait until Georgie moved into a dorm.

Anna had roasted two marshmallows at a time, one on each prong of her fork. She was good at it, turning the fork slowly while the marshmallows became golden brown, hot and ready to ooze with creamy goodness.

And wasn't that the wrong image to entertain when he had a traumatized kid hiding under a blanket? When it came to sex, a toddler worked better than a chastity belt. He should keep that in mind. Nothing would happen with Anna while Georgie was around.

He finished his s'mores and reached for another marshmallow. "At this rate I'll end up eating twice as many as you."

She arched a brow. "I'm going for quality, not quantity."

"Ever eaten a burnt one?"

"More than I wanted to. I burned plenty as a kid and sometimes while helping Georgie. I prefer this kind."

"Are they done yet, Mama?" Movement under the blanket indicated someone was getting impatient.

"Almost, son."

Garrett skewered another one and held it over the fire. "How does Georgie like his marshmallows?"

"Lightly toasted."

"Want s'mores, Mama." Georgie lifted a corner of the blanket.

"Would you like to help? You can put the chocolate on the graham cracker so it's ready when I finish roasting your marshmallow. If you make two like that, we can eat these at the same time."

No response from under the blanket. But there was subtle movement. Garrett glanced away. Georgie wasn't much different from a colt who'd been mistreated early in life. Or a boy.

Garrett recognized the fear and distrust, another reason he was the right man to help Georgie lose it. If he didn't look at the kid, Georgie might hold onto his illusion of invisibility, even without the blanket.

Sure enough, the swish of the blanket and the scrape of a cracker on a plate told him Georgie had slid out from the safety of his cocoon and was arranging the crackers and chocolate. His breathing was fast, like he was working quickly so he could dive back under the blanket when he was done.

Garrett continued to gaze in the opposite direction. Maybe he'd hit on a partial solution for sharing space with this little guy. If so, then—

His phone chimed. He'd left it on the kitchen table. Henri's ring. Odd, since she'd talked with Anna not long ago. If it was a small matter, she would have texted him.

"Excuse me a minute," he murmured. "I'd better take this."

The blanket rustled. No doubt Georgie was back under it. That was a shame. Laying his fork with a slightly-warmed marshmallow on the hearth, he headed for the table and picked up his phone. "Hey, Henri."

"Are you available?"

"Um... yes, ma'am." Henri didn't ask on the spur-of-the-moment unless it was critical.

"Good. Then please come up to the house as soon as you can. A cowboy claiming to be Jake's half-brother just arrived."

\* \* \*

Garrett told Anna what Henri had said, added her phone number to his phone contacts and promised to be in touch. Then he lit out.

The drive to the main house took about five minutes and he packed that time with a million unanswerable questions. Jake had mentioned that his folks had married and divorced each other several times. His mom had often accused his dad of carrying on with other women during the periods when they were divorced.

But Jake had cut off contact with his dysfunctional parents quite a while ago. Although the possibility of a half-brother existed, for him to show up here, to even know where to look for Jake, was unlikely. Was it a scam of some sort?

Jake's truck wasn't parked in front of Henri's so he and Millie hadn't arrived yet. Garrett considered waiting for him and decided against it. Henri needed backup. She had Ben there, but maybe that wasn't enough.

Being summoned to aid Henri was a privilege he didn't take lightly. She leaned on him more these days, possibly because he was the only unattached wrangler on the ranch, the man she could call on because she wouldn't be dragging him away from his sweetheart.

Her trust and maternal affection filled a void he hadn't acknowledged until coming to work at the Buckskin. Like the other members of the Brotherhood, he'd had a lousy childhood. Henri was the parent he'd longed for. He'd do anything for her.

An unfamiliar truck sat next to Ben's. Must belong to this supposed half-brother. It was covered in dried mud, bits of ice and slush. Clearly it had been on the highway for a couple of days, maybe more. The license plate was obscured with muck, too. No telling where this guy hailed from.

Garrett took the porch steps two at a time and went inside without knocking. That was another privilege he didn't take lightly.

Leaving his hat on the ornate coat tree in the entry, he unbuttoned his coat but left it on as he walked into the living room. He might need to invite this guy outside for a serious discussion.

They were all standing in a loose circle, and the stranger had on his coat, too, but his hat was in his hand. At least he had some manners. And... what the hell? Who was the little blond girl? She looked to be around eight, dressed in jeans, boots and a bright red parka.

Everyone turned in his direction and Henri came toward him. "Garrett, I'd like you to meet Zeke Lassiter and his daughter Claire. Zeke and Claire, this is Garrett Whittaker, one of our wranglers and a trusted friend."

Zeke held out his hand. "Pleased to meet you, Garrett."

Garrett formed his first impression of folks by their grip during a handshake. Zeke had a good one, firm without being aggressive. That didn't mean he was legit, but it was a start.

The guy had said the accepted thing, that he was pleased to meet him. He opened his mouth to say... something that wasn't a lie. He wasn't pleased to meet this guy. He was concerned about his sudden appearance and worried that he had an angle of some kind. What to say in response?

Then his daughter thrust out her hand. "Pleased to meet you, Mr. Whittaker."

He shook her hand. Whatever was going on, it wasn't her doing. "Pleased to meet you, too, Miss Lassiter."

"You can call me Claire. But I'm supposed to call you *Mister* Whittaker because you're an adult. I'm just a kid."

"A very polite kid."

"Thank you. My daddy taught me how to speak to adults. He says they deserve my respect, unless they turn out to be jerks. Then I'm not supposed to talk to them at all. I can give them the cold shoulder."

"I sure wouldn't want to get the cold shoulder."

"You won't. I can already tell you're not a jerk. You're a cowboy."

"Yes, ma'am." He gave her a smile and gazed at Zeke. A guy with a little girl like Claire couldn't be all bad.

The front door opened and Millie came straight into the living room without pausing, followed by Jake, who grabbed his hat from his head as he barreled into the room. He looked like he was ready to hit something. Or somebody.

He screeched to a halt, his eyes widening. "My God." He sucked in a breath. "You look just like him."

"My misfortune." Zeke stared back, turning his hat in his hands, nervously fingering the brim. "I hope you won't hold that against me."

Henri glanced from one to the other. "I guess that answers the question of whether Zeke's telling the truth."

Jake nodded, his expression stunned. "He is." His attention shifted to Claire. "Your daughter?"

"Yes. This is Claire." He put a hand on her shoulder.

"I...I can't..." Jake continued to stare, clearly at a loss for words.

Tense silence reigned until Henri broke it. "Zeke asked if I can use his help on the ranch. The fact is, I can, since you're so busy with Raptors Rise these days. But it's your call."

Jake took another deep breath. Then he studied his half-brother for several seconds. "We..." He paused to clear his throat. "We set a high standard at the Buckskin. We're a close-knit group. I'm okay with Henri giving you a chance, but unless you're willing to work hard and pull your weight, you being my half-brother means nothing."

"I'll work hard. I'll do whatever needs doing. I want to stay. I want to get to know you, Jake. I want Claire to get to know you."

The little girl gave him a smile.

Jake's breath hitched. "Hello, Claire."

"Hello, Uncle Jake."

"That brings us to the next decision." Henri turned to Garrett. "Zeke figured on staying in the bunkhouse."

"That's fine. Plenty of beds."

"Claire wants to stay there, too."

His jaw dropped. "But—"

"I promise I won't be any trouble, Mr. Whittaker." Her words came in a rush, her expression eager. "I'll keep out of your way, unless you need me to help with something. I'm a good helper and I've always wanted—"

"Claire, you and your daddy are welcome to stay with us," Millie said. "It's not a bunkhouse, but it *is* a log cabin. We don't exactly have a guest room yet, but we can figure something out." She glanced at Jake, who nodded.

"Thank you, ma'am, but I'm going to be a wrangler like my daddy when I grow up. I've always wanted to live in a real bunkhouse with real cowboys." She turned back to Garrett. "I'll do my part with the chores. I'm good at chores. Please say it's okay. *Please.*"

He was at a loss. A little girl in the bunkhouse? It would require some major changes in protocol. Increased modesty, for one thing. Monitoring language for another.

What about the Brotherhood overnights? She'd have to stay with Henri for those. No way should an innocent kid be present for that kind of blowout.

"We could try it for a while, at least." Henri gave him a quick smile. "See how it goes."

"Yes, ma'am." And that was that. Life as he knew it was officially over.

# 6

Anna never had trouble getting Georgie up and dressed for daycare. He loved Erica, the woman who ran it, and the kids he played with, especially Carl. Thank goodness she could afford it. The socialization was so good for him.

When she'd explained that Henri would be giving them a ride this morning, he powered through his breakfast, too. Miss 'enri was coming.

He sounded like a British kid when he said her name. She'd made a good impression from the get-go, and a ride in her truck added extra excitement to Georgie's day.

"When is Miss 'enri coming, Mama?"

"In about two minutes." She was eager to see Henri, too. Garrett had texted her the night before. Jake's half-brother had moved into the bunkhouse, along with the guy's eight-year-old daughter. Anna wanted to know more of the story.

She tugged Georgie into his blue hooded snowsuit and zipped it up. "We'll wait on the porch."

"Yep." He started for the door.

"Hang on. Wait for Mama." He was all about doors since he'd grown tall enough to turn the knob.

"Wanna go out."

"In a minute." He couldn't reach the deadbolt, which was her saving grace.

Taking her parka off the coat tree, she shoved her arms into the sleeves and grabbed the duffle bag containing a change of clothes in case he spilled something on what he was wearing. His to-go bag was less complicated now that he was potty-trained.

She looped her purse over her shoulder and checked to make sure her keys were inside.

Georgie jiggled in place by the door. "Come *on.* Miss 'enri's coming!"

"Okay. I'm ready." She walked to the door, flicked the deadbolt and put her hand on the knob. "Don't run out on the porch. Remember what happened yesterday."

"I felled down."

"What are you going to do today?"

He sighed in resignation. "Go slow."

"That's right. Me, too. It's icy and slippery."

"Heat Miser could melt it, Mama!"

"He sure could. Too bad he's not here." A week before Christmas, Carl's mom had loaned her an old DVD of *The Year Without a Santa Claus.* He'd watched it at least a hundred times.

He'd expected that version of Santa to show up at his house. Instead, Santa had turned out to be a full-grown man, much taller and more imposing than the jolly fellow in the movie. Only the familiar outfit and the promise of a little moose had kept him out on the porch that night.

No sooner had she shepherded Georgie out the door and locked up than Henri drove in, her headlights sweeping the front parking area. Technically the sun was up, but it was still hidden behind the mountains.

The cabin's front-porch light illuminated Henri's buckskin-tan long-bed sporting a ranch logo on the side panel of the front passenger door. The truck was only a few months old and Henri was proud of it.

"It's Miss 'enri!" Georgie would have bounded down the steps if she hadn't put a hand on his shoulder.

"Easy does it, son."

Henri swung down from the cab and rounded the front of the truck, her boots cracking the frozen ground under her feet. "Good morning! Didn't expect to find you waiting on the porch."

"I didn't want to put you out any more than necessary."

"Like I said last night, this gives me another chance to spend time with Georgie." She paused at the bottom of the steps and met his gaze. "How're you doing, cowboy?"

"Cowboy?"

"You're not a cowboy?"

"No."

Anna gave him a nudge.

"No, *ma'am*."

"I would've sworn you were. Do you want to be one?"

Georgie turned back to Anna, looking for guidance.

"You'd make a great cowboy," she said. "If that's what you want."

"I only ask because..." Henri crouched down and pulled a toddler-sized Stetson from behind her back. "I happen to have this in case you'd like to have it."

Anna gasped. "Henri, that's adorable, but I'll pay you for—"

"It's my gift to Georgie, if he wants it. All the wranglers wear a hat like this. I thought he might like one, too."

Georgie came to the edge of the steps and squatted in an exact mimic of Henri as he studied the hat. "Grit has one, Mama."

"Yes, he does, son."

Henri glanced at Anna. "Grit?"

"Garrett. He calls him Grit."

"I see." Amusement danced in her eyes as her attention shifted to Georgie. "You don't have to take it if you don't want to. I just thought—"

"I want it." He held out one pudgy hand.

"Then it's yours. Would you like help putting it on?"

"No."

"Georgie—"

"No, ma'am." He took the hat and crammed it on over his snowsuit hood.

Henri grinned. "That works."

"Say thank you, son."

"Thank you, Miss 'enri."

"You're welcome, Georgie. It suits you." She stood and turned to Anna. "How will we work this between here and your car, when we pick up his car seat?"

"Yesterday I held him on my lap and Garrett belted us in together."

"Then we'll do that. Approximately where is—"

"Just beyond that sharp curve at the bottom of the hill."

"Got it. Let's go."

Belting the two of them in together wasn't as smooth now that Georgie was wearing a cowboy hat. He didn't care for the idea of taking it off, either. Anna settled him as best she could. The brim of the hat poked her in the chest, but it wouldn't be for long.

Once Henri pulled away from the cabin, Anna finally had a moment to ask about Jake's half-brother. "Garrett texted me that he has roommates again."

Henri chuckled. "Yes, he does. Zeke Lassiter and his daughter Claire. She's a pip. Garrett wasn't too sure about having her in the bunkhouse, but I predict she'll have him wrapped around her little finger in no time."

"How's Jake doing? He had to be blindsided."

"He was, but there's no doubt Zeke's his half-brother. Evidently he's the spitting image of their father when he was younger."

"I don't get to spit," Georgie mumbled.

"*Spitting image* is an expression," Anna said. "It means two people look alike."

"Do they spit?"

"I doubt it."

"Miss 'enri said they spit."

"But she didn't mean it that way. It's—"

"*I* don't get to spit."

Henri murmured *sorry* under her breath.

"It's fine."

"Hey, Georgie." Henri glanced at him. "What's your favorite thing to do?"

"Make 'mores."

"I like that, too."

"Grit maked 'mores."

"Did you do that with him last night?"

Georgie hesitated. "No."

Anna gave him a nudge.

"No, *ma'am*. Mama, why can't I spit?"

"It's bad manners."

"Carl spits."

"Yes, and Carl's mama doesn't like it. She's told him not to."

"But he *spits*. He—"

"Why don't you tell Miss Henri about your moose?"

"You have a moose, Georgie?"

"Yes." He took a quick breath. "Yes, ma'am."

"Does your moose have a name?"

"Carl."

"You must have named your moose after your friend."

"Yep."

"I have a moose."

"You do?" The brim of Georgie's hat scraped across Anna's chest as he turned to gawk at Henri. "From Santa?"

"Yes, as a matter of fact. From Santa. I named my moose Ben."

"Can I see him?"

"Sure. Come to my house sometime and I'll show you."

"Mama, can we go?"

"We'll find a time."

"Can I take Carl?"

"You mean your moose?"

"Yep. He wants to go."

"Then we should arrange a meeting between Ben and Carl," Henri said. "Your mama and I will set it up."

"Okay!"

"The curve's just ahead. Your car's just beyond that, you said?"

"Off on the left-hand side."

Henri slowed as she rounded the curve. "This curve is tricky after a storm."

"Especially if you can't slow down. There's my car." She sucked in a breath as it came into view.

Henri eased up on the gas and glanced over. "Oh, honey." She put on the brakes and turned on her blinkers. "That makes my tummy clench."

"Mine too. It looks worse than I remembered."

"Put your faith in Garrett. He's a good mechanic. I didn't realize that until recently when CJ needed some work done on his aging truck and Garrett offered to help. CJ couldn't say enough about Garrett's expertise."

"That's good to know."

"Grit maked the fire."

Henri looked at Georgie. "In your cabin?"

"Yep. My house. I don't want—"

"Come on, Georgie. Let's go get your car seat. You don't want to be late for school."

"Yes, ma'am."

# 7

Short on sleep and jacked-up on caffeine, Garrett took the shortcut through ranch property on his way to fetch Jake from Raptors Rise. Ranch guests were directed to take this back way, too, but the general public accessed the sanctuary from the main entrance off the highway.

Jake usually finished cleaning the raptor enclosures around ten, so Garrett pulled up in front of the visitor center a little before that. He had to get the car keys from Anna and arriving early might give him a chance to talk with her.

A silver-haired couple stood at the desk buying their tickets. Visitors could make a reservation for a guided tour with Jake or just show up and use headphones and a recorded narration for a self-tour of the sanctuary.

Nobody had scheduled a guided tour for this morning, so Jake was at liberty to help pull Anna's car out of the snowbank. He likely could use some hard labor and a member of the Brotherhood who'd be a good listener. Garrett could supply both.

The couple picked up their equipment for the self-guided tour and headed off. Garrett smiled at Anna. "How are you this morning? Any lingering aches or pains?"

"Not a one, thank goodness."

"Good to hear. You look right at home behind that desk."

"I am. Don't you love this building? You'd swear it was an old ranch house, complete with a porch and rockers where folks have been sitting for generations."

"I do love this building, although I doubt you'll have many porch sitters until the weather warms up."

"Probably not, but when it does, I think Jake should consider having a food concession. Something simple, like snacks and lemonade or iced tea."

"Great idea." And she looked amazing in a yellow Raptors Rise logo turtleneck. She'd worn her hair down, a sleek, dark curtain that brushed her shoulders. "Did you have on a logo shirt yesterday?"

"No. I leave my supply of shirts here and change before I start work. Then I change back before I pick up Georgie. He has a talent for getting stuff on my clothes and some of it doesn't come off easily, like glue."

"The shirt looks nice on you. Especially that cheerful yellow."

"Thanks." Her cheeks turned a sweet shade of pink. Dropping her gaze, she took her purse out from under the counter. "I put the car key on a separate keychain so you can keep it as long as you need to."

"Let's hope that's not very long." He pocketed the key. "I'll text you once I have something to report."

"I'll keep my phone handy. I appreciate you and Jake doing this, especially considering the new development with his half-brother."

"I figure he'll relish working off some steam."

"No kidding. I haven't had a chance to talk with him yet. He had no idea this guy existed?"

"None."

"I'll bet you had an interesting night, too."

"Yes, ma'am."

"Won't that be difficult, having Claire in the bunkhouse? I haven't been in it, but I doubt it's kid-friendly."

"It's not. But she has her heart set on living there, so we'll adjust."

"Since you'll have more on your plate, now, you're welcome to back out of our deal."

Was she looking for an excuse? "I don't plan to." He paused. "Unless you've changed your mind."

She gazed at him and sighed. "It's not that I've changed my mind. I just don't think it'll be much fun for you."

"I had a good time last night. His Captain Invisible routine is funny." And he had no problem taking guff from Georgie if it meant spending time with her.

"It'll be an uphill battle, I'm afraid."

"Maybe not. I think we've made progress already."

"I'd hoped so, too. But this morning he was ready to tell Henri he doesn't want you in his house. I didn't let him finish the sentence, but that's where he was going with it."

"Does Henri know the issue?"

"She does, now. I filled her in on the way back from town and mentioned that you'd offered to help."

"What does she think?" If Henri questioned the plan, he'd pull back.

"She said I couldn't find a better man for the job."

Warmth filled his chest. "Nice of her to say."

"She thinks the world of you, Garrett. She praised your mechanical skills, too."

"Wow." He grinned. "The pressure's on."

"I worry about that. She said when you take on a job, you see it through."

"That's generally true." He'd had no idea Henri had such a high opinion of him, though. Gratifying. And humbling.

"That tells me you'll soldier on no matter how challenging the task is, whether it's my car or my son. You could end up with a lot of grief in both cases."

"I can take it. I like challenges." But he'd be a fool to minimize this one. He was confident he could fix her car given enough time. He was fairly certain he could win Georgie's trust if he kept at it. The kid's curiosity would eventually melt his resistance. The third goal, winning Anna's trust, would be the toughest hill to climb.

"Hey, there's the man of the hour!" Shearling coat unbuttoned, Jake walked into the reception area from a hallway to the right. The rooms in that direction included an office, an infirmary and a nursery for orphaned baby birds who would need shelter come spring. "Got that bunkhouse situation under control?"

"Not even close, bro." How he loved calling Jake that. Maybe eventually he'd take it for granted, but he hadn't yet. "Have you talked to Zeke?"

"Considered texting him this morning. Decided to wait until I'd talked with you. How did it go?"

"Well, I'm in love."

"Me, too. The jury's still out on whether Zeke gets to stay, but Claire's in, for sure. That kid is awesome. She'll be barrel racing with the Babes before you know it."

"Yeah, she will. She was up before dawn, bouncing around, raring to go to the barn. I took the two of them down there and you'd think she was headed to Disneyland." A barn visit was another avenue he wanted to explore with Georgie. Most kids loved being around horses.

"That's very cool. Well, guess we might as well get going." He buttoned his jacket and flashed Anna a grin. "It's all yours. Have that donation bucket filled by the time I get back."

She smiled. "No problem."

"I know. That's why I said it." He glanced at Garrett. "Donations have picked up substantially since Anna came on board. She coaxes money out of visitors like you wouldn't believe."

"I do believe it. And that reminds me." Garrett reached for the wallet in his back pocket. He'd intended to put some money in the bucket and talking with Anna had made him forget.

"That comment wasn't meant to nudge you into contributing, bro," Jake said. "You already gave me a nice check this month. Don't—"

"I want to." He folded a twenty and shoved it through the slot in the bucket on the counter.

"Well, thank you." Jake gave his shoulder a squeeze. "Let's move out before you divest yourself of any more of your hard-earned cash. B-bye, Anna." He made for the door.

Garrett followed. "I'll text you," he called over his shoulder.

"I'll watch for it. And thanks for the donation."

"Welcome." He went out the door Jake held for him.

Jake lowered his voice. "You like her a lot."

"How can you tell?"

Jake rolled his eyes and set off for Garrett's truck. "Let me count the ways. One, the lovesick expression on your freshly shaven mug when I walked into the reception area. Two, the gallant gesture of stuffing a twenty in the donation bucket when a five would have done just fine. Three, the lilt in your voice when you said *I'll text you* and the unspoken endearment that lingered in the air."

"There was no unspoken endearment." He walked quickly around to the driver's side and climbed in.

Jake swung into the passenger seat, shut the door and buckled up. "For the record, I think she kinda likes you, too."

"Seems like it, but she's not dating anyone until Georgie's in college." He started the truck and backed out.

"While I admire that on one level because she's thinking of her kid, I'd hate to see her wait for years when she has a good guy like you on the hook."

"I'm not—"

"Yes, you are."

"Yeah, okay. I am." He headed back the way he'd come.

"I could talk to her. I stalled way too long before I worked up the courage to date Millie, and I regret those lost years."

"Don't talk to her. She has a good reason not to date. Georgie hates guys."

"I know he doesn't like me, but I thought I'd screwed up somehow."

"He doesn't like men, period."

"Her ex's doing?"

"Bingo."

"You plan to work on that issue?"

"I do."

"The good news is she got her son away from the bastard at a young age. Georgie might not end up totally jacked the way most of us did."

"And speaking of that. I got a little info on Zeke's ex-wife. She's no prize, either."

"Are you saying Zeke gets the credit for that amazing kid?"

"Could be."

"Huh. That's a point in his favor. I sure wish he didn't look exactly like my father did at thirty. Dear old dad was a heartbreaker. Broke mine, too."

"It's not Zeke's fault."

"I know that, but I still have the urge to punch him in his disgustingly handsome face."

"Just focus on Claire, then. We need to decide what horse to start her on."

"She doesn't ride? And she wants to be a wrangler?"

"Her mom put the kibosh on that dream. Refused to let her near a stable."

"That sucks. How the hell did a woman who hates stables and horses end up with my brother... I mean, *half*-brother?"

"Just so you know, he's not making that distinction anymore. He probably felt he had to when he first talked to Henri, but ever since he and Claire arrived at the bunkhouse, he's called you *my brother* or if he's talking to Claire, it's *Uncle Jake.* Oh, and she's decided all the members of the Brotherhood are her uncles."

"She's right. I can't wait for everybody to meet her." He stared out the front windshield for a few moments. Then he glanced over. "Did Zeke say why he split with this woman? And how he got custody?"

"He couldn't go into it because Claire was with us, but he did say the judge gave him sole custody."

"Which is unusual, especially with a daughter, but clearly that was the right call. She adores him."

"Henri seemed to take a liking to him, too. She has good instincts."

Jake nodded. "She can spot a wounded soul at fifty paces." He sighed. "So can I. Do you suppose he's known about me all these years?"

"I doubt it. I get the impression he just found out recently."

"Must've been my wedding, then."

"Your wedding?"

"Millie thought I should let my mom know about it. After the fact, I mean. I didn't want her showing up here on New Year's Eve. But I sent a note to her the first week in January. She must've told my dad, who evidently decided to spill the beans to Zeke."

"Possible."

"Although I don't see why my marriage would prompt him to tell Zeke about me."

"Maybe because you're more stable than Zeke is right now. You could be a steadying influence on him and Claire."

"If you're implying my dad's thinking of someone besides himself—"

"He's Claire's grandfather. Is it such a stretch that he could be worried about her since her parents have split up?"

"Yes. Yes, it is. He's never—"

"People change."

"I know, but—" He glanced past Garrett as they rounded the curve and Anna's car came into view. "Holy hell. She buried that car good, didn't she?"

"She was going fast when she hit."

"Gives me the gollywobbles just looking at it."

"Me, too. But she says she's okay." He checked his rearview mirror before pulling across the road. Then he backed up until he was only a couple of feet from her car. "I guess my point about Zeke is that he seems like a decent guy. And Claire will be fun to have around."

"Millie has the same opinion as you. She wants to get to know Claire better. She's planning to invite her along when she has afternoon tea with Kate today."

"I guarantee Claire will love that. I'm glad Millie thought to ask her right away. Tomorrow Zeke's enrolling her in Apple Grove Elementary so her weekdays will be taken up."

"He's putting her in school already?"

"Yep. As far as he's concerned, they're staying."

"I see." Jake cleared his throat. "Then I guess I'd better get acquainted with them."

# _8_

A busy morning kept Anna from obsessing about her car, but she kept glancing at her phone in case Garrett texted.

Instead he walked in with Jake. Luckily they showed up when nobody was standing at the reception desk in need of attention.

Jake split off and headed down the hallway. "Gotta check on that injured golden."

"Thanks for the help, bro." Garrett pulled off his gloves and tipped back his hat as he approached the reception desk. "I decided it was silly to text since I was bringing Jake back. Your car's going to be fine."

"Fine? Really?" Relief flooded through her. "It's not out of alignment?"

"I can't tell that for sure until I drive it, but we'll think positive that the snow was fluffy enough that it's okay. The bumper's scratched up a bit because there was some gravel mixed in with the snow but the headlights didn't break."

"That's very good news." And he sure looked good delivering it. The cold had brushed his cheeks with color that emphasized the aquamarine sparkle of his eyes. "Where is it?"

"We towed it to the parking area of the bunkhouse. I can work on it there this afternoon. It's a decent day for it, no wind, sunny."

"I'm glad for that."

"I hope to have it done so you can drive it tomorrow, but I'll plan to fix the bumper on a day you don't need to use the car."

"Does the bumper affect the way it runs?"

"Not really. It's cosmetic."

"Then we can leave it as is."

"No need to do that. It won't cost you anything."

"What do you mean?"

"It's all labor. Well, except for a can of touch-up paint. That's not much."

"It costs *you*, though. Your time is worth something."

"Like I said, I enjoy the work. Restoring that bumper would make me happy."

"Are you sure?"

"Yes, ma'am."

"Then thank you. But just the bumper, okay? Promise me you won't go looking for other dings."

He hesitated.

"I mean it, Garrett."

"All right, I promise."

"Do you still want to come for dinner?"

"I'd love to."

"I can't guarantee that Georgie will—"

"No parent can guarantee their child will be well-behaved. Not any good parent anyway. Which lets out the ones who rule with an iron fist."

The muscles around his eyes tightened. A subtle tell.

Had he had such a parent? "I'm making meatloaf, if that works for you—"

"I love meatloaf. Are we doing s'mores for dessert?"

"If you don't mind. It gives us another chance to get Georgie involved."

"Mind?" He chuckled. "Can't ever have too many s'mores."

"Alrighty then." His enthusiasm was catching. "The meatloaf will be done around six."

"If I show up at five-thirty, can I help you with the side dishes?"

"Absolutely."

"Then I'll be there at five-thirty. If I can drive your car over, I will. But you'll need Millie to give you a ride into town this afternoon to fetch Georgie."

"Henri wants to do it. She talked Millie out of the job."

"Figures. She's a sucker for kids and Georgie is cuter than the devil."

She laughed. "Except when he *is* a devil."

"Even then. I worry him, but I fascinate him, too."

Perfect description of the effect he had on her, too. "Why do you say that?"

"His urge to spy on us."

"Good point. That's something new. He's never done that spying business before."

"Here's my theory. Because I'm a man, he's conditioned to expect me to behave a certain way. But I don't follow the pattern. So he's curious, but wary. Any minute I could change and start acting like his father."

Especially if he kissed her. No wonder Georgie had yelled at them. Her ex would make sexual advances when he wanted to take her attention away from their son. She'd resist, inciting one of Brad's tantrums.

"Are you okay?"

She blinked and drew in a breath. "Yeah. I just...had a flashback."

"You looked like you wanted to light into someone and I can guess who. Is this plan stirring things up?"

She met his worried gaze. "It is, but that's my problem, not yours. I haven't invited a man into my personal space since the divorce. Georgie's not the only one who has to get used to the idea."

"I know." His voice was gentle. "Still want me there?"

"Yes. Just so you understand that I—"

"I understand, Anna. I'd never want to cause you distress. See you at five-thirty." Touching two fingers to the brim of his hat, he turned and walked to the door. He didn't look back.

She, on the other hand, followed his every movement as his long strides took him across the lobby. He pulled the heavy door open with ease and stepped outside.

A group of three older women approached the entrance. He must have greeted them, because they paused to chat, smiling at something he'd said. He held the door for them before walking briskly to his truck.

"What a perfect start to our visit," one of the women said to the other two as they approached the reception desk. She sounded like she might be from back East, maybe Boston.

"No kidding," another one said with the same accent. "Our first real cowboy."

The third woman grinned. "And a dashingly handsome one at that." She glanced at Anna. "Do you know that man?"

"Yes, ma'am. He's one of the wranglers at the Buckskin."

"Do the other ranch hands look like him?"

"I'm probably prejudiced, but I think they're all very attractive."

The woman turned to her two companions. "We screwed up, girls. We should have booked a cabin here at the ranch instead of getting rooms at the hotel in town."

Jake picked that moment to walk down the hall and into the lobby, still wearing his shearling coat and his Stetson. "Hello, ladies." He tipped his hat in their direction. "Welcome to Raptors Rise. What can I do for you on this lovely afternoon?"

"Definitely screwed up," the first woman muttered under her breath.

Anna swallowed her laughter as Jake laid on the charm. In a matter of minutes, the ladies had cancelled their hotel rooms, booked a large guest cabin, paid for a personal tour and made a generous donation to the sanctuary.

They'd also given her a renewed appreciation for her circumstances. They were visitors, while she was one of the lucky women who lived here surrounded by the good guys of the

Buckskin Brotherhood. Instead of recalling past traumas, she'd be better off counting her blessings. And Garrett was certainly one of them.

\* \* \*

Garrett added to her already high opinion of him when he pulled up to her cottage driving her Taurus.

At the rumble of a car's engine, Georgie ran to the window. He was still wearing the cowboy hat Henri had given him. She'd mentioned that a cowboy usually took off his hat indoors, but he'd looked so crestfallen she hadn't insisted on it.

He pushed the curtain aside, stood on tiptoe and pressed his face to the window. "Mama! My car! It's back!" Then his jubilation turned to dismay. "Grit? Grit's got my car?"

"It needed to be fixed, son. Garrett fixed it for us."

"No! He can't fixed it!" He whirled away from the window. "He can't fixed it, Mama!" He sent her a pleading look.

"He can and he did. We're fortunate that he—"

"Don't *want* him." The sound of a car door opening sent him racing back to the window. "He's coming! Grit's coming!"

"I invited him for dinner."

"No!" Georgie ran to the door and hopped up and down trying to reach the deadbolt.

"Georgie. Son. Take it easy." She walked over and laid her hands on his shoulders. "He's coming for dinner and then we'll have s'mores."

He stopped jumping, clearly torn by opposing desires.

Garrett tapped on the door.

That settled the matter. "Don't want Grit, Mama." Georgie took off for the safety of his room.

She sighed and opened the front door.

"Alignment's fine and brakes are operational."

"That's awesome!" Garrett's pleased expression almost cancelled out Georgie's negativity.

"Zeke pitched in, which made things move along faster."

"That sure was nice. Would you tell him thank you for me?"

"Happy to. So far, he's been an asset around here."

"I'm glad to hear it." She peered around him. The car was a lot cleaner than it had been when she'd driven it yesterday. "Don't tell me you washed it, too."

He shrugged. "Made it easier to evaluate the damage to the bumper."

"Let me get my coat. I want to check that out." She plucked it from the coat tree and shoved one arm in the sleeve as she came out the door and closed it behind her.

"Hold on." He grasped the hood, helped her into the other sleeve and settled the parka over her shoulders.

"Thanks." The slight pressure from his hands gave her the tingles. The urge to have body contact with the guy was becoming annoyingly frequent. She held the parka closed instead of bothering to zip it. "I don't remember my car being that shiny even after I washed it." She descended the steps.

"I happened to have some wax."

She turned back as he came down behind her. "You *waxed* it? Garrett!"

He gave her a little-boy grin. "Told you I like messing with vehicles. Making them run better. And look better."

"Well, my car hasn't looked this good since I bought it. Thank you." She crouched to examine the bumper. "These few little pock marks and scratches? That's what you want to take care of?"

"Wouldn't you rather not have them?"

She stood and faced him. His eyes gleamed with eagerness. "You won't be happy unless you complete the job, will you?"

"No, ma'am. It's a good little car. No reason for it to have dings in the front fender."

"All right, then. I appreciate all your effort."

"You're very welcome." He held up her keyring. "Normally I'd suggest going for a test drive, but that's complicated."

"Uh, yeah. And I just thought of something. If you drove my car over here, how are you getting back to the bunkhouse?"

"I'll walk."

"That seems wrong."

"I'm not asking you to drag Georgie along, especially because it'll be close to his bedtime."

"I know, but—"

"Zeke offered to come and get me if I need a ride."

"Then I want you to contact him when we're finished with the s'mores. It's too cold for you to walk."

"No, it's not, but I'll text him later if that will make you feel better."

"It will. And thank you again. The car looks great."

"You're so welcome."

A breeze picked up and she shivered. "Let's go in. It's another good night for a fire."

"And s'mores."

"Absolutely." She led the way into the house. A quick glance confirmed that Georgie had shut his door. "I'm thrilled to have my car back so soon, too." She hung up her parka. "Your speedy job calls for a bottle of cider."

"I accept." He left his coat and hat on the coat tree and followed her into the kitchen nook. "I see Georgie's door's closed."

"He wasn't happy that you fixed *his* car. But you know what? I'm not going to insist on him leaving his door open or try to coax him out. You just did us a huge favor and if he doesn't appreciate it, too bad."

"I was glad to do it."

"I can tell, which makes the gesture even more special." She took two bottles of cider out of the fridge. "You'd better have come prepared with a bill for the parts, though."

"I did." He pulled it out of his shirt pocket and gestured toward the bottles in her hand. "I'll open those while you look at the bill."

"Thanks." She gave him the bottles and took the receipt. Her eyes widened as she glanced at it. "That's it?"

He shrugged. "The parts aren't that expensive."

"But the labor is." She gazed at him. "A meatloaf dinner doesn't seem adequate. I should have picked up some steaks or—"

"A meatloaf takes more effort than a steak."

"Yeah, but—"

"Anna, I enjoyed doing you this favor."

"You've said that and I understand that you like working on vehicles. But I feel the need to reciprocate."

"Clearly you haven't read the latest research on happiness."

"Probably not."

"Fortunately, I have." He handed her one of the bottles. "Doing nice things for others is one of the key ingredients. This repair job borders on selfish, because I enjoy the work and it's a big help to you."

She smiled. "I don't think selfishness figures into it."

His cheerful expression disappeared and he glanced down, clearly uncomfortable.

"Garrett? What's wrong?"

He raised his head and met her gaze. "Selfishness does figure into it, Anna." He hesitated. "I'm attracted to you."

She gulped. "But I thought we agreed that—"

"We did, and I promise to abide by your rules. But in all fairness, I should admit that I'm hoping someday you'll bend those rules."

Her chest tightened and breathing became difficult. "You don't know what you're asking."

"Maybe not, but I'm trying my best to understand. You've given me hints of the hell you've been through. And then there's Georgie."

"And he's the most important person in my world."

"As well he should be."

She searched his expression, her heart thumping. "Do you mean that?"

"I do. He was here first. He has claim to your unwavering allegiance."

The tension in her chest eased. "Thank you for that." She soaked up the compassion in his beautiful eyes. "Since we're confessing things, I should admit I'm attracted to you, too."

His breath caught. "Thank you for telling me."

"It might not be the right thing to do. I don't want to give you false hope."

"Doesn't seem false. More like a glimmer of light in a dark tunnel. I'll take it."

The glow of pleasure in his eyes had a hypnotic effect. She moved closer. "But since Georgie resists the idea of having a man around, there's no way I can—"

"I know that." He reached out to touch her cheek and pulled back. "It's okay. First things first."

"Thank you." She appreciated his restraint. She really did. But she longed for him to stroke her cheek. Just once.

# 9

Anna wanted him. Could it be that he'd finally found the right woman? He dived into food prep as if he'd dismissed the topic of their mutual attraction, but he hadn't, not by a long shot.

While he tore lettuce and sliced tomatoes, while he steamed veggies and sautéed garlic in olive oil, he continued to savor the moment when she'd told him, her eyes bright and her cheeks flushed. He'd barely stopped himself from touching her.

Good thing he'd restrained the impulse. Brushing his hand over her warm skin wouldn't be enough. He'd want to taste her full lips. That would be a betrayal.

She'd trusted him enough to share her feelings. She'd already stated her reservations. Kissing her would be unfair.

He only had one path forward, making friends with Georgie. The little boy's door remained firmly closed. Evidently, driving up in the car Georgie considered his private property had crossed a line.

*No good deed goes unpunished.* He'd heard that years ago, long before he'd read the article about happiness. He should contact the psychologist who'd written the article and ask about the saying.

Anna grabbed a couple of potholders and took the meatloaf out of the oven.

"Smells wonderful." Not as wonderful as she did, some spicy perfume he'd guess had been recently applied. He'd keep that observation to himself.

"Thank you. I like this recipe." She set the dish on a hot pad and took plates from the cupboard. "Georgie hasn't come out to spy on us, which tells me he's super upset. I'm going to take his food into his room and close the door when I leave."

"All right."

"I'll have a little chat with him when I do that. He's being rude to someone who's been nothing but kind to him. Maybe I can bring him around."

"Maybe. But seeing me driving the car seems to have really bothered him."

"Apparently." She cut a small piece from the meatloaf and put it on one of the plates. "Much as I hated having the accident, it was a good thing. I have a bigger problem with Georgie than I realized if he can't handle you driving our car."

"He's just afraid. I'm invading his world and that scares him."

"I know, but if we don't deal with it now, it'll only get worse."

His heart warmed. She'd used *we.* She'd included him.

She put salad and a helping of vegetables on his plate. "Since he'll probably eat in his room, what would you think about moving the table over behind the couch? Then we can watch the fire while we eat."

"Good idea. I'll set us up while you take his food in."

"Thanks." She sent him a smile as she poured a glass of milk and got child-sized silverware out of a drawer.

While she put everything on a tray, he crossed to the table, picked it up and carried it over to the couch. When he turned around, she'd paused with the tray in her hands. She looked momentarily disconcerted as she focused on him.

He glanced back at the table. "Isn't that where you wanted it?"

"You put it in exactly the right place. I just… I'd forgotten what it's like to have a man around who can move things without effort."

"It's not heavy. I'm sure you could—"

"I could. And I have. But my arms are shorter than yours and so is my body. I can't accomplish the task as elegantly as you just did."

He snorted. "I wouldn't call that move elegant."

"Well, it was." She headed toward Georgie's room.

*Elegant?* No way. The slight sway of her hips as she walked toward Georgie's room, though—that was elegant. Poetry in motion.

Carrying the table was no big deal. But evidently she'd enjoyed watching him do it. Good sign that she was becoming aware of—

"I think we'll need more firewood." She balanced the tray against her hip and reached for the doorknob. She glanced over her shoulder. "There's more under a tarp beside the porch if you'd be willing to get it."

He snapped out of his daze. "Sure thing." Time to cool the hell down. He decided against putting on his coat as he walked outside to fetch the wood.

There was nothing sexy about her request to fill the wood box, but the gleam in her eyes just now had sent a distinct signal to his privates. He knew that expression, and it meant a woman was beginning to contemplate the possibilities.

She might deny it, but what had prompted her suggestion to set up closer to the fire? A lot more romantic than the kitchen nook, right? At least he considered it romantic. She might just like the warmth of the fire.

He loaded up on wood and was nicely chilled by the time he came back in. The firm tone of her voice penetrated the closed door of Georgie's room, but not the words themselves. He felt for the little kid. Change was hard.

Once the fire was crackling, he brought two chairs over and positioned them on either side of the table. Then he took silverware out of the drawer, found where she kept the napkins and set two places.

The fire could use another log. He was adding one when she came out of Georgie's room alone.

"You're right about the car being the problem," she said. "He had trouble expressing it, but he's convinced you're taking charge of everything and on some level he remembers that wasn't a good thing in the past."

"Any idea how we can show him I'm not taking charge?"

"We can hold off on the bumper repair, for one thing. I know you're itching to make it look good again, but—"

"Not if the car's a bone of contention. That repair can wait. Ready to have some dinner?"

"Yes, I am." She walked toward the kitchen. "I don't eat by the fire often enough. Maybe I should just leave the table there for the rest of the winter." She picked up a plate and dished herself some food.

"I would." He started filling his plate.

"Be sure you take plenty."

He chuckled. "Yes, ma'am. I got that memo." He carried his food over to the table.

She set her plate down and headed back to the kitchen. "I'm going to have another bottle of cider. Would you like one, too?"

"Sure. I'm not driving tonight." He followed her back to the fridge and took the bottles she handed out to him.

"I can't believe two bottles of cider would affect you."

"Probably not." He opened both and gave one back. "It's just one of those things people say."

"In my case, it applies." She carried her cider back to the table. "If I had to drive, I wouldn't have another. But I'm ready to take the edge off reality for a little while."

"Don't blame you." He helped her into her chair. If they'd been alone in the cabin, he would have taken her statement as a hint that she was open to some cuddling by the fire. But they weren't alone. Still, it meant she trusted him enough to let down her guard.

He glanced at the fire before sitting down. "Think I'll shift those logs around, make sure they've all caught. I'm going for a nice bed of coals, unless you've changed your mind about s'mores."

"Not at all."

"Good." He rounded the couch and crouched in front of the fire. "I'm looking forward to 'em."

"Me, too. I told Georgie we'd be doing it. I can't imagine he'd pass that up, but who knows? He has a stubborn streak."

Garrett smiled. Like his mama? Not a bad thing. No doubt it had fueled her determination to get out of her bad marriage.

"You seem to know your way around a fireplace."

"Not until I hired on here. The fire pit out behind the bunkhouse is where I learned the most about building and maintaining one."

"Jake said that's a popular gathering place. Do you think having Claire living with you will change that?"

"Some." He came back to the table and pulled out his chair. "But from what I hear, it's been changing, anyway. Guys are finding sweethearts who are now part of the mix. CJ and Isabel's baby won't stay a baby. Before we know it, Cleo Marie will be dancing around the fire like her mama."

"You guys dance out there?"

"As best we can, considering our dance floor is a section of trampled grass. When CJ starts playing a lively two-step, nobody can resist."

Her expression grew wistful. "I can picture it."

"If we can get Georgie over his issues, you'd be welcome to bring him to one of the gatherings."

"That's a big *if.* He loves to dance, though."

"He does?"

She picked up her fork. "I suppose that's hard for you to picture since you've only seen him when he's upset. But it's adorable." She took a bite of meatloaf.

"What does he like to dance to?"

She chewed and swallowed. "Country songs. Erica, the woman who runs the daycare, shows the kids videos of country dancing and coaxes them to mimic the steps. They do a pretty good job. I'm prejudiced, but I think Georgie's the best."

"I'd like to see that." When she talked about her son in a positive context, her face lit up and her eyes sparkled. What a treat. "This meatloaf's amazing, by the way."

"Thank you. It turned out even better than usual." She hesitated. "Do you really want to see him dance?"

"I do, but there's no way he'll come out and demonstrate."

"I took a video of him the other day. I'll get my phone." She left the table, went over to the coat tree and dug it out of her purse.

He put down his fork as she came around to his side of the table.

She scrolled through her phone. "Here it is." Instead of handing it to him, she stood by his shoulder and leaned down, holding it so they both could see the screen.

He understood the impulse to watch it with him. But the combination of her warm breath on his cheek and the scent of her spicy perfume played hell with his concentration.

Okay, he could do this. The tune was George Strait's *All My Exes Live in Texas*, and Georgie zig-zagged around the room, executing a credible two-step with an imaginary partner.

He chuckled. "I'll be damned. That's beyond cute."

"Apparently today he insisted on wearing his cowboy hat while they danced. I wasn't there in time to catch that."

Her voice was pitched low since she was so close. If he turned his head... nope, not going there. "He has a hat?"

"Henri gave it to him this morning." The video ended and she straightened. "He's had it on all day." Returning to her seat, she started eating again.

He managed to take a deep breath and let it out without being obvious. "That's terrific about the hat. If he wants to be a cowboy, then—"

"I don't know if he does or not. I think the appeal of the hat is that Miss 'enri gave it to him."

"He says her name like that?" He tucked into his food, too. "With a British accent?"

"That's how it comes out. By the time he says *Miss* he doesn't have enough breath to make the H sound."

Garrett gazed at her. "The Brotherhood would fall in love with your little guy, Anna."

"So how do we get him to fall in love with them?"

"I'm not sure, yet, but he has all the makings of a little cowpoke. He has the hat and he loves to dance. All he needs is a pair of boots and... hey, wait a minute. He had on boots when Santa paid him a visit at Christmastime."

"Yes, he did, which is how he managed to nail Leo. That outfit was borrowed, and the boots were a little small for him, anyway."

"What size shoe does he wear?"

She stopped eating and gave him a long look. "I'm not telling you."

"He doesn't have to know they're from me, and if he loves his new hat so much, then he'd probably—"

"That's not the point. I don't want you spending that kind of money."

"It would be fun for me."

"He'll outgrow them in a few months."

"He'll outgrow the hat, too."

"That was a done deal. Henri had already bought it. Asking her to take it back would have been rude. And not to be indelicate, but she has more money to throw around than you do."

"Not necessarily."

"I'm not saying she's filthy rich. She has plenty of overhead. But unless you have money stashed away and you're just working here for fun, chances are she can afford a hat more than you can afford a pair of leather boots for a toddler."

"Maybe I don't have Henri's financial resources, but I make decent money and not much to spend it on. I could easily afford—"

"No, Garrett. It's a very generous offer, but I can't let you do it."

"All right." Then he flashed her a smile. "You said his birthday's in May. Can I get him boots for his birthday?"

She laughed. "We'll see. You're worse than Georgie when he gets an idea in his head."

"I just think he'd look cute wearing them. Uh-oh, I'd better tend to the fire." He left the table and rounded the couch. Crouching on the hearth, he rearranged the logs and replaced the tongs in the holder. "How does Georgie feel about horses?"

"I don't think he's ever been close to a real one. Why?"

He returned to his seat. "Easing him into ranch life might be a way to go. Kids are usually fascinated, especially if they're introduced to a gentle horse to begin with."

"Um, okay." Not exactly an enthusiastic response.

"How do *you* feel about horses?"

"I don't know. I don't have any experience with them, either."

"You don't? I don't know why I thought—"

"My ex was the one who was gung-ho to live in Montana. I spent my whole life in Indianapolis."

"Why didn't you go back?"

"Didn't want to. Ironically, he insisted on moving here and I'm the one who adores the place. Love the mountains and this little town. Besides that, I don't exactly fit in with my family."

"I know how that is."

"They think I was crazy to get a divorce. They predicted I'd struggle financially. Brad has a talent for making money, and because he was a good provider, I was supposed to *work it out.*" She added air quotes.

His jaw tightened. "Good thing you didn't try."

"That's for sure. He caused enough damage as it is."

"Okay, I have an idea. It'll be better if you get acquainted with a few of the horses before we try it with Georgie. How about having lunch with me at the barn tomorrow? I'll introduce you around."

"To the wranglers? I think I've met most of—"

"To some horses. I'll pack sandwiches and bring a thermos of coffee."

She met his gaze with the same look that earlier had telegraphed interest in getting chummy. "Sounds like fun."

Oh, yeah. It would be.

# *10*

Georgie wasn't the only one who was afraid of losing control. Anna was right there with him. Garrett had a way about him. She'd set boundaries, and he was a man of honor. He'd abide by them. But would she?

Garrett had charm to burn and her trusty chaperone was AWOL. While they finished their dinner, Garrett gave her a run-down on the horses stabled in the barn. Normally all of them would be in the pasture that time of day, but he'd bring in three, each distinctively different, for her first meet and greet.

He described them with an affection similar to the way she talked about Georgie. His enthusiasm was endearing. Sexy.

How was she supposed to resist him? He'd fixed her car and stood ready to help fix her son, too. He wanted to buy Georgie boots and teach him to be a cowboy.

But she needed to resist this knight in shining armor, at least for now. Her son still distrusted men and getting involved with one would blow his mind. He'd see it as defecting to the enemy.

By the time they'd finished eating and organized everything for s'mores, Georgie hadn't come out. She glanced at Garrett standing near the fire waiting for her decision on whether to start. "I'll go invite him one more time and see if maybe he'll decide to join us."

"By all means."

She couldn't ask for a more understanding man to navigate these tricky waters with Georgie. Or a more appealing one... aughhh! She shoved her inappropriate impulses away, walked over to Georgie's door and tapped on it. "Hey, son."

"Don't want Grit, Mama."

"Okay. But I need to get your dishes." She opened the door and stepped into the room. Her chest tightened. Georgie was so alone in there. "We'd like you to come out and make s'mores with us."

The look he gave her broke her heart. She battled the urge to tell him she'd send Garrett away. But then what? Georgie would never dance by the fire pit, would never know that Garrett and the Brotherhood were friends to be cherished, not enemies to despise. "You're not coming out?"

He didn't answer, just looked at her, his dark gaze stubborn and unyielding.

"We'll miss you." She picked up his dishes and left the room, closing the door behind her. She carried the dishes to the kitchen nook, swamped by the pain of her child's unhappiness.

"Anna."

Garrett was right behind her.

She set the dishes on the counter. "He won't..." No reason to finish the sentence.

Garrett put his hands on her shoulders and turned her to face him. "I'll leave if you want me to."

"I don't want you to." The warmth of his hands on her shoulders spread, soothing her anxiety and replacing it with something much nicer.

Lifting both hands, she rested them lightly on his chest. Ah, that felt so good—wear-softened cotton plaid over solid muscle. She focused on the steady movement beneath her palms as he breathed.

Gradually his breathing changed and his grip on her shoulders tightened. He swallowed. "Anna."

She raised her head and met his gaze.

"Do you want me to kiss you?"

"Yes."

Heat flared in his blue-green eyes. "Are you sure?"

"Yes."

Slowly he lowered his head, giving her plenty of time to change her mind.

She wasn't about to. He wouldn't take it too far. He wasn't the type to throw caution to the winds. Maybe this would be their one and only kiss. But it was one they both wanted, both needed. She closed her eyes.

His mouth brushed over hers, gentle as a warm breeze. Then he drew back. Was that it? Please don't let that be all he'd allow himself. She hadn't specified the type of kiss she was looking for, but more than that, for heaven's—

He touched down again, the velvet texture of his mouth firm against hers, his fingers flexing, drawing her closer. His lips parted, coaxed hers to open. Moist heat sent urges spiraling to her core. She clutched the front of his shirt.

And he pulled away.

She whimpered.

He came back. Lifted her to her toes. This time he settled his mouth over hers with deliberate intent. Wooing her with teasing, sensuous movements of his lips that stole her breath, he gradually built the tension in her eager body.

She whimpered again, wanting... *yes!* He claimed her with a firm thrust of his tongue and a soft groan that spoke of desperation tightly leashed.

Sinking beneath a wave of pleasure, she abandoned herself to a kiss she never wanted to end.

But it did. He eased back with such tenderness that tears threatened. She blinked them away and gulped. "Th-thank you."

"Ah, Anna." Releasing his hold on her shoulders, he wrapped her in his arms and cradled her against his broad chest. "I'm the thankful one." His voice was husky. "I thought it could be weeks. Months."

She took a shaky breath and nestled her cheek against the soft cotton of his shirt. "I weakened."

"You're not weak." He stroked her back. "You're human."

"Guess so."

"So am I. And that's why I'm going to leave without making s'mores."

"You are?" She looked up. "But you were looking forward to—"

"If I stay, I'll want to kiss you again."

The warmth in his gaze created a delicious quiver deep in her core. "Fine with me."

"I'd rather quit while I'm ahead."

That made her smile. "Are you ahead?"

"I think so. You let me kiss you long before I thought you would." He glanced toward Georgie's room. "And if I leave now, it'll be our little secret."

She sighed. "Good point."

"Letting go of you will be tough, though." He pulled her closer. "This feels very good."

"Sure does."

He took a deep breath and let it out. "But I'm leaving." He loosened his grip and stepped back. "Have a s'more for me."

"I will." She fought the urge to reach for him.

He walked over to the coat rack and unhooked his jacket. "So I'll see you down at the barn around noon tomorrow?"

"For what?"

He grinned. "Lunch and your meet and greet with the horses." Lifting his hat from the coat tree, he settled it on his head.

"Oh. I forgot all about it."

"I'll take that as a compliment."

"It was."

"See you then." He touched two fingers to the brim of his hat and opened the front door.

"Wait! You didn't text Zeke!"

"I know. The walk will do me good."

"But it's so cold out there!"

He laughed. "Exactly."

Gone. She wrapped her arms around her middle and hugged herself. Not quite the same, was it?

She hadn't been kissed like that in... oh, who was she kidding? She'd never been kissed like that. Back in high school, she and her friends had discussed which of their boyfriends were the best kissers.

Some of the girls had rhapsodized about the wonders of a great kiss. She'd figured they were making it up. Or that she had impossibly high standards that no man could achieve.

Wrong-o. Garrett Whittaker had nailed it on the first try. Her mouth still tingled and the rest of her was party-ready, too. He was likely in the same shape since he'd chosen to walk home.

Now what? She didn't regret that amazing kiss, not for a second, but she'd further complicated what was already a minefield. Now that she'd tasted her first Garrett kiss, she'd be craving another one. Judging from what he'd just said, he would be only too ready to oblige, but—

"Where's Grit?"

She turned.

Georgie stood just outside his door, his slightly too-big cowboy hat pulled over the tips of his ears as he searched the area, poised to dash back inside.

She took a deep breath. "He's gone home."

"To his house?"

"To the bunkhouse."

"What?"

"A bunkhouse is where cowboys live."

"Oh." He ventured out and peered at the fixings for s'mores sitting on the folding table. "Will he comed back?"

"Not tonight."

"But he didn't maked 'mores."

"No."

"Why?"

"It's complicated."

"I wanna maked 'mores."

Technically she shouldn't let him. But technically she shouldn't have kissed Garrett, either. "Okay, let's do that."

## 11

The scent of wood smoke drifted toward Garrett as he neared the bunkhouse, which was lit up like a Christmas tree. Jake's truck sat in the parking area along with Rafe's.

Last night Zeke had asked where to put his mud-spattered rig. Garrett had suggested parking near the front door. It looked a whole lot better sitting there now than it had last night. Today Zeke had washed it, revealing a new dark green paint job on an older-model F150.

Zeke kept his truck in good shape, which earned Garrett's respect. The guy's help with Anna's car had been valuable, too. Garrett was glad to see Jake's truck here. He must be making good on his plan to get acquainted with his new-found brother and niece.

What a great kid Claire was, and what a treat watching her walk into the bunkhouse last night. She'd surveyed the bunks lining either side of the main room and the antique wood stove across from the front door. Then she'd lifted her gaze to the weathered rafters and glanced over her shoulder toward the kitchen. Finally, she'd turned to her father with a grin that took over her entire face. "It's absolutely perfect, Daddy."

Game over. Garrett had exchanged a glance with Zeke, their unspoken agreement clear. They'd do whatever was necessary to make the new living arrangement work for Claire.

When he opened the front door, her perky voice rang out from the kitchen. "Is that you, Uncle Garrett?"

"Yes, ma'am." Good thing he'd become part of the Brotherhood in December, for many reasons. Being Claire's uncle was the latest and promised to be an important one.

"Daddy, one more game, so Uncle Garrett can play?"

"One more. Then it's bedtime."

Garrett left his coat and hat in the bunkroom, walked into the kitchen and evaluated the distribution of chips on the table.

"Play at your own risk," Jake said. "It's open season on the hombres tonight. The ladies are cleaning our clocks."

"I can see that."

"Look at my stash, Uncle Garrett." Claire gestured toward the respectable number of chips in front of her.

"Nice."

"Aunt Kate has the most, but that's okay. She's been playing longer than me."

"So have I, cutie-pie," Jake said. "How do you explain my sorry performance?"

Claire gazed at him. "Aunt Millie said you've allowed yourself to become distracted."

Jake busted out laughing. "Your Aunt Millie's a smart woman."

"I know."

Zeke picked up his phone from the table. "Did I miss your text, Garrett? I thought you were going to—"

"I was, but then I felt like walking."

Jake glanced at him. "Everything okay?"

"Everything's fine. Anna was thrilled to get her car back so soon." He looked at Zeke. "She asked me to thank you for helping out."

"My pleasure."

"Good thing you got here before nine, Uncle Garrett, 'cause that's my bedtime. But we can squeeze in one more game. You want to play, right?"

"Sure. What's the buy-in?"

"Twenty-five cents, but if you don't have it, I'll make you a loan. Interest-free."

"That's very generous, but I think I have it." He dug a quarter out of his pocket. "Who's the banker?"

"Me." She held out her hand. "You can sit right there next to Uncle Rafe. Maybe you'll bring him luck."

"I'd be honored if you'd sit by me, bro. Heard about your heroic deed yesterday."

"What heroic deed?" Claire gave him his chips.

"It's nothing." He took the chips. "What are we playing?"

"Up to Claire," Kate said. "She's the dealer this round."

"Texas Hold 'Em." She shuffled with surprising skill for her age. "Twos are wild." She passed the deck to Jake to cut the cards. "I still want to know about this heroic deed."

"The one we told you about when we had tea," Kate said. "Uncle Garrett saved the day when Anna's brakes failed."

"That was you?" She beamed at him. "That's cool! I've heard so many Buckskin Ranch stories today that they're all a mish-mash in my brain." She took back the cards from Jake, got to her knees on the chair to give herself a longer reach, and began to deal. "I'll get them straight eventually."

"I have no doubt." He was thoroughly entertained by this self-possessed little girl. "Who taught you to play poker?"

"My daddy. I had to talk him into it. But I'm going to be a wrangler, and everybody knows they play poker." She proceeded to direct the game with the poise of a professional and won the hand.

After collecting her chips, she gazed at her father. "Daddy, can we play one—"

"No, honey. That's it. Go brush your teeth and put on your PJs. I'll be there in a few minutes to tuck you in."

"Yes, sir." She slid off her chair and made the rounds, hugging everyone goodnight.

Zeke gazed after her, love and pride shining in his expression. Then he turned back to the group and lowered his voice. "I want to thank you for making my daughter's dreams come true."

Jake chuckled. "She dreamed of poker?"

"Not just poker. Playing a game in a bunkhouse like this one." He glanced at Millie and Kate. "You two are a bonus. She couldn't stop talking about the tea party. She raved about the flowered teapot from England, the taste of loose-leaf tea with honey, the brownies, the pretty napkins. She loved everything."

"She's like a sponge," Millie said. "I can't wait for her to watch a barrel racing demonstration by the Babes."

"Oh, my God, that'll be epic," Kate said. "But be prepared, Zeke, because she's going to want to be a barrel racer, too. I can smell it coming. Save your pennies."

"Oh, I will. But first she has to learn to ride."

"Garrett and I talked about that today," Jake said. "When you're ready to start the lessons, Lucky Ducky is your best bet. We'll get with you and figure out a practice schedule."

"I'd appreciate that." He held Jake's gaze. "I appreciate everything. I couldn't ask for a better..." He paused and cleared his throat. "You've all been great to my daughter."

"It's easy," Jake said. "She's amazing."

Zeke swallowed. "Yes, yes, she is." He pushed back his chair. "I'd better go hurry her along."

After he left, Garrett looked over at Jake. "How's it going, bro?"

He took a shaky breath. "I still see my dad every time I look at him, but I'm losing the urge to punch him."

"That's progress."

"Evidently my dad took up with his mom right after I was born. Zeke's only a year younger than me."

"Was your wedding the reason he found out about you?"

"Yep. My mom told him I was happily married and he decided Millie and I could be a support system for Zeke and Claire. You were right about that."

"Then does your mom know about Zeke, now?"

"No, she does not. My dad asked her for my address so he could send Millie and me a wedding present."

"Which he did," Millie said. "I'm reserving judgment about Zeke until I get to know him better, but Claire's definitely a gift."

Kate nodded. "For sure. This afternoon she was super careful with the teacups and saucers. When I let her pour, she treated it like an enormous privilege."

"She's easy to love, all right." Garrett couldn't help contrasting her behavior with Georgie's. He sighed. "Too bad Georgie isn't more like her."

Rafe gave him a nudge. "Has he kicked you in the privates, yet?"

"He wouldn't kick me on purpose." He hesitated. "At least I don't think so."

"He wouldn't," Millie said. "I haven't seen any aggression when he comes into the visitor center with Anna. Just avoidance. He stays far away from Jake."

"Hurt my feelings, too," Jake said. "Until I found out he doesn't like Garrett, either. Or any man."

Rafe grew more alert. "Sounds like a problem with the father."

"Yep." Garrett relayed what he knew about Anna's ex.

Rafe swore softly. Then he dragged in a breath and scrubbed a hand over his face. "I hate hearing that kind of thing." His gaze took in the men at the table. "Guess we all do."

"Yeah," Jake said, "but in this case, we might be able to repair the damage while he's still young." He glanced at Garrett. "When I asked you how it was going, you said fine."

"I didn't want to get into it right then, but things didn't go well with Georgie. He stayed in his room the whole time I was there."

"Did things go well with Anna, then?" Jake smiled.

"None of your business."

"Just wondering if that's why you looked so pleased with yourself when you walked in."

"Aha." Rafe pointed a finger at him. "Now I get the picture. I thought I detected a gleam in your eye."

"That's a side issue. I—"

"A side issue?" Millie gave him the stink-eye. "Are you calling Anna a side issue?"

"No, I just—"

"Seems to me it's all the same issue. One created by her miserable ex."

He gazed at Millie. "You're right, as usual. I stand corrected."

"The problem isn't complicated." Millie neatened up her stack of chips. "But it is tough. Convincing Anna and her son that you can be trusted won't be easy."

"And if I can't make progress with Georgie, I'm finished. He doubled down tonight, wouldn't come out of his room at all."

Millie gave him a sympathetic glance. "That's a shame."

"I thought of one way to go. He loves the Stetson Henri gave him today and he likes dancing to country music. I think with a little encouragement he might decide he wants to be a cowboy."

"Unless his dad's one," Jake said.

"He isn't. That's kind of where I'm going with this—cowboys have a reputation as the good guys."

"Come to think of it," Rafe said, "that was a big draw for me."

"Same here." Garrett glanced around the table. "So is the concept solid?"

"It's good," Millie said. "But how do you plan to go about it?"

"I want to start with Anna."

Jake laughed. "I'm guessing you've already *started* with Anna."

"That's not what I mean."

"Am I wrong?"

"Never mind. The point is, I'm meeting her at the barn tomorrow during her lunch hour."

"Are you, now?"

"It's not what you're thinking. Ultimately I'd like Georgie to visit the barn and pet the horses.

But Anna needs to take him down there and she's never been around a stable. I want her to feel confident so Georgie will, too."

Jake smirked.

"Cut it out, Jake. I'm introducing her to the horses and providing lunch. That's it."

"Uh-huh. Just keep in mind she only has an hour break."

Millie smacked him on the arm. "Garrett's come up with an excellent idea for initiating this plan. Don't tease him."

"Millie, darling, it's what I do. And if Garrett spends almost an hour with Anna in a barn that's largely deserted that time of day, and he doesn't take the opportunity provided, he's not the man I think he is."

"Then I suggest you give Anna an extra half-hour for her lunch break."

"Excellent idea." Jake winked at him.

Garrett ducked his head to hide a grin. The trip to the barn was for Anna and Georgie's benefit, but the place usually was quiet around noon.

Jake's teasing had sparked an idea. If he passed the word around that he'd appreciate having some privacy during the lunch hour, he could guarantee nobody would show up. Under those circumstances, what would be the harm in stealing a kiss or two?

# _12_

The temperature dipped the next morning and a blustery wind blew in heavy gray clouds that promised snow. The clouds had settled into the canyons of the jagged mountain range by the time Anna left the visitor center for her lunch date with Garrett. It likely wouldn't start snowing before she came back.

Tucking her wool scarf around her neck, she pulled up her parka hood and put on her gloves before climbing in the car. She'd changed out of her Raptors Rise shirt into the one she'd wear later to pick up Georgie. She'd also put on her snow boots. Jake had said her loafers would be fine, but she wasn't taking any chances. It was a barn, after all.

The double doors of the hip-roofed barn were closed when she drove into the clearing. Garrett was waiting for her, leaning against the weathered wood, one booted foot propped against it, his hat nudged back and his hands shoved in the pockets of his shearling coat.

He smiled, drawing her attention to the lips that had driven her to distraction last night. She gulped. He wouldn't kiss her in broad daylight, though. Anyone could come along.

Yeah, kissing would not be happening. What a relief. And a disappointment? Yes, much as she hated to admit it. The prospect of another kiss had been niggling at her all morning.

But the barn was a critical feature of this ranch. The other wranglers would be around... wrangling.

Pushing away from the wall, Garrett ambled toward her. No trucks were parked near the barn, leaving her unsure where she should put her car. She didn't want to take someone else's spot. Someone who could drive up any minute.

She braked, rolled down her window and called to him. "Where should I park?"

"Just pull straight ahead." He gestured toward the barn. "Keep going until your tires touch that pole staked to the ground."

"Got it." She rolled up the window.

He followed her over, walking along beside the car. When she switched off the engine, he reached for the door handle and pulled. Then he rapped on the window.

Déjà vu. She hit the unlock button and he opened the door.

She glanced up at him. "Sorry. Habit."

He extended his hand. "Left over from the big city?"

"I guess." She put her hand in his and wished she'd taken her gloves off after turning off the engine. But even with them on, she registered a zing of pleasure as his fingers tightened around hers. "Normally I have Georgie in the car and locking all the doors feels safer."

"I'm sure it does." He helped her out.

When he released her hand, she took off her gloves and shoved them in her pocket. "Locking the front doors makes no sense, though. He's in the back seat which has child-proof locks."

His expression gentled. "If it feels safer to you, then go for it."

"Maybe as he gets older I won't be so paranoid." Turning, she pushed the door shut.

"I wouldn't call it paranoid. You're solely responsible for a very young child."

"True." What a feast for the eyes he was. She'd better not spend too much time looking at him, though. Every time she did her pulse rate spiked.

"That places quite a burden on your shoulders."

The compassion in his soft-spoken words prompted her to admit something she rarely told anyone. "I can't count how many times I've been terrified of making the wrong decision. And if I do, the consequences will be..." She took a shaky breath. "Awful."

"But you've made a lot of good decisions."

"Thank you." Was kissing him one of them? Or a huge mistake? Either way, she needed to stop looking at his tempting mouth.

"Ready for your barn tour?"

Barn tour. Right. "Absolutely."

He held out his hand. "Then let's get started."

She hesitated, in debate mode once again.

"Would you rather not hold my hand?"

She looked up. "It's just that I...."

He waited, his gaze patient.

"Holding your hand isn't such a big deal, is it?"

His eyes sparkled with amusement. "I don't know. Is it?"

"No." She slipped her fingers through his. And wasn't that lovely? Warmth traveled up her arm and fanned out in anticipation of more sensual stimulation. Ah, she was traveling a tricky path.

"Let's go visit some horses." Tightening his grip, he led her toward the heavy double doors, grasped the handle of the one on the right and effortlessly slid it open. Awareness curled in her belly.

She stepped inside and he pushed the door shut, enclosing them in cozy warmth surrounded by a pleasant scent like cut grass. Electrified antique lanterns hanging from the beams bathed the wooden interior in a retro glow.

Clearly he'd put time into arranging their lunch venue. Next to the stall on her left, two stacked hay bales were draped with a red checkered cloth and places had been set. A tree stump on either side of the makeshift table provided rustic seating.

She glanced back at him. "And I thought you'd just hand me a sandwich you grabbed out of a cooler. This is very nice." And romantic.

"I wanted your first-ever barn visit to be special."

"Is that why Jake insisted on giving me an extra half-hour for lunch? He knew what you were up to?"

"Um, more or less." His lips twitched as if he was trying not to laugh.

*Was* he planning to kiss her during this barn tour? The signs were beginning to point in that direction.

He cleared his throat and gestured behind her. "Lucky Ducky's impatient to meet you."

She turned and came eye-to-eye with a good-sized brown horse who'd poked his nose over the stall door. "I see what you mean about the white patch on his forehead. It does look like a four-leaf clover."

"It's worked for him, too. He's led a charmed life."

"Is that so, Lucky Ducky?"

The horse regarded her solemnly for a moment before stretching his nose in her direction. She backed up and stepped on Garrett's boots. "Whoops, sorry."

"No problem. You okay?"

"He startled me when he did that."

"He's hoping you'll give him a piece of carrot."

"Was I supposed to bring one?"

"No, ma'am." He reached around her, a chunk of carrot resting on his palm. "Hold it just like this and he'll nibble it off your hand."

She plucked the carrot from his palm. "He won't bite me?"

"He's an herbivore. He prefers carrots to fingers."

The rumble of his voice just behind her shoulder sent shivers up her spine. "Good to know."

"He's a sweetheart. He was here when Lucy started coming to the Buckskin with her folks years ago. He was the first horse she rode. He's still her favorite."

"How old is he?"

"Henri's not sure. Past thirty. He owes his longevity to the nutritious carrots people feed him. Hint, hint."

"I'm getting there." She positioned the chunk of carrot on her palm the way he'd shown her, moved forward and held out the carrot.

"Closer. Don't make him strain to get it." Garrett put a hand at her waist and gave her a subtle nudge.

Her slight quiver had nothing to do with the horse and everything to do with the virile man and the warmth of his touch.

She took another step and extended her arm. Lucky Ducky lowered his lips to her palm and nuzzled it gently.

Her breath hitched. "Tickles."

"See how gently he scooped it up?"

"See how big his teeth are?"

"I'm not saying horses don't bite. Some do if they've had poor training or have been abused. We don't have any biters. Want to give him another one?"

"Okay." She fed Lucky a second piece of carrot and he repeated the same routine, his mouth brushing lightly over her palm as he gathered up his treat. This was becoming fun. "How about one more?"

"Two's enough for now. We can give him more when we come back to eat our lunch. But petting him would be good. He likes that, too."

"I don't know how a horse likes to be petted."

"I'll show you." He drew her closer to the stall. "He enjoys having his neck stroked and scratched. Most horses do. Like this." He rubbed a hand over the animal's powerful neck before curving his fingers and giving him a slow scratch.

A shudder of pleasure rippled through Lucky's body. If Garrett did that to her, she'd probably respond the same way.

"You try it."

She laid her palm on the horse's neck. "His coat's softer than I expected."

"He gets brushed every day. They all do."

"No wonder he looks so good for his age." She stroked his warm, muscular neck. Then she tried the scratching routine and he shuddered again. "He really likes this."

"Sure does."

"I'll bet he's glad to be in the barn where it's warm."

"He probably is, considering his age. But Prince and Thunderbolt would rather be outside running around."

"In this weather?"

"Yes, ma'am. They all grow a winter coat so they're ready for it. It may be warmer in here, but it's boring to be stuck inside."

"You'll turn the other two loose after I've met them?"

"Thought I would."

"Then let's move on so they can enjoy their freedom." She gave Lucky a pat and backed away from the stall. "See you later, okay?"

The horse bobbed his head and made a soft *huh-huh-huh* sound.

She looked at Garrett. "Is he talking to me?"

"Yes, ma'am. He just told you he likes your company and you're welcome to drop by anytime."

"That's very nice." She gave her new equine friend a smile. "Thanks, Lucky. I like you, too." Then she turned to Garrett. "Who's next?"

"Thunderbolt." He set off for the far end of the barn. "We'll stop at Prince's stall on the way back."

"Prince looks friendly, too. He's watching us go by. Why is he wearing... is that called a halter or a bridle?"

"A halter, and both he and Thunderbolt have one on so I can quickly get them back outside."

"Did you bring carrots for the other two?"

"I did."

"Thunderbolt must not have gotten the word. He hasn't stuck his head out like Lucky and Prince."

"Because he's not the warm and fuzzy type. But you won't find a more magnificent horse."

"That's what Jake told me. He said Thunderbolt has been a good investment for Matt."

"That's for sure. He's brought in some respectable stud fees."

"I gathered that." She had questions about how horse breeding worked these days, but she'd ask somebody else, not the man who was currently holding her hand, the man she longed to kiss and... engage in other... yeah, not a good topic to broach with Garrett.

A hot topic, too. She unzipped her parka with her free hand. No need to bundle up when holding hands with this cowboy.

He paused in front of Thunderbolt's stall. "Hey, Thunder," he crooned. "How's it going?"

The stallion tossed his mane and pawed a furrow in the straw beneath his hoof.

Anna stared up at him, awestruck. "He's *huge.*"

"Tallest horse in the stable." Garrett chuckled. "Matt likes pointing that out."

"That black coat makes him seem even more imposing, especially when he arches his neck."

"He's a looker, all right. And the foals he's sired are good-looking, too." Garrett's voice dropped into the velvet tones he'd used initially. "Gonna come see us, big guy?"

The massive stallion snorted, and Anna jumped back.

"It's okay." Garrett glanced at her. "He's high-spirited, but he's not dangerous."

"I'd still rather watch from a distance."

"You bet." Garrett squeezed her hand and let go. Then he moved closer to the stall. "Evidently he's not in the mood to be sociable, anyway." He pulled a chunk of carrot from his pocket and balanced it in the middle of his palm. "Peace offering, Thunder. I know you didn't want to come in. I'll take you out in a little bit."

The stallion pranced forward, took the carrot and backed away again. Garrett laughed. "Yeah, he's holding a grudge because I took him away from the herd."

"Are mares in the pasture?"

"Yes, ma'am."

"Don't you have to keep him in a separate pen from them?"

"Not this time of year. But in the spring, yes, we do." He came over and took her hand before starting back the way they'd come. "Last of all, I want you to meet Prince, Henri's pride and joy. You can feed him carrots just like you did Lucky."

"He does look mellow." Anna had researched Buckskins after she'd been offered the job here. Prince had the classic buff-colored coat paired with a black mane and tail. "So where is everybody?"

"What do you mean?"

"With so many cowboys working here, I expected to see—"

"Nothing much to do right now. The stalls are mucked out and none of the guests are excited to book a ride on a day like this."

"I'm not surprised. I can't believe Thunderbolt and Prince want to be out in it." Maybe nobody would show up, after all. She and Garrett might end up alone here for the next hour. Her stomach fluttered.

"Most horses will take a chilly wind if it means they have space to roam and interact with the rest of the herd." He stopped in front of Prince's stall. "Thanks for waiting for us so patiently, buddy. Anna has something for you." He handed her a piece of carrot.

"Here you go, Prince." She held her palm flat and the horse nibbled it delicately the same way Lucky had. When he'd finished his second one, she moved closer and gave him some rubs and scratches.

"You've got the idea," Garrett said. "Next thing you know you'll want to try riding."

"I wouldn't mind, but Georgie complicates the situation." She gave Prince one last scratch. "See you later, sweetie. I'm turning you over to Garrett so he can take you and Thunderbolt outside." Stepping back, she waved at Prince. "He's all yours."

"I'll take him out and go fetch Thunder." He reached for a rope hanging near the stall. "You'll want to move to the far side of the aisle."

"Will do." She was unclear about the process of getting the horses out of the barn, but she was more than happy to stand back and let Garrett handle it.

After he brought Prince out and secured the lead rope, he started back to Thunderbolt's stall.

Prince cast a glance in her direction.

"Thanks for coming in so I could meet you, Prince."

His ears pricked forward and he made the same low-throated noise Lucky had.

She smiled. "We'll meet again. I—" She paused and moved closer to the wall as Garrett headed in her direction, a prancing Thunder close behind him.

"Having a conversation with the big guy?" Garrett untied Prince's lead rope.

"A short one."

"I'm sure he appreciates the attention. You can follow me down to our lunch spot, but just like driving, keep a horse-length distance." He led both horses toward the entrance.

She stayed well back as she walked behind them. When Garrett opened the doors, she braced for a blast of wind that never came. Instead, fat snowflakes drifted down and caught the light from inside the barn.

"Garrett, shouldn't you bring the horses back in? And go get the others?"

"No need. They don't mind a little snow. Be back in a bit." He led the horses out and circled them back around so he could close the doors.

She glanced over at Lucky Ducky, who had his head over the stall door, watching the proceedings. "I don't know much about horses, Lucky, but I know something about men. I think that cowboy was hoping the barn would be deserted. Our being here alone isn't exactly an accident, is it?"

The horse gave her a blank stare.

"You probably don't want to squeal on him, but I'll bet he mentioned something to you when he was arranging the table. His job involves keeping track of the weather, so he knew that would be in his favor, too."

Lucky's low-pitched groan sounded like a confirmation of her suspicions.

"I'm going to flat-out ask him when he gets back. Maybe it's pure coincidence that we happen to be all alone here—well, except for you—but if he set up this equine meet and greet just so we could be alone, then—" She turned as one of the double doors opened.

Garrett slipped through it quickly, shoving it back in place. "I have a confession." He hooked the ropes over a nearby peg and left his hat there, too.

She faced him, heart racing. "This is a setup?"

"It didn't start out that way. But then Jake pointed out that usually nobody's around during the noon hour." He unbuttoned his coat as he came toward her. "Which made me start thinking about the possibilities."

She gulped. "I see."

"All I ask is a kiss. Just one. I haven't been able to think of much else since last night."

"Me, either." She took a shaky breath.

"It turns out we are alone, at least for now, and that's not likely to happen very often. I desperately want to kiss you again."

She met his gaze. The heat in his eyes reduced any hesitation to ash.

He rested his hands on her shoulders. "Yes or no?"

She wanted him so much she was quivering. "Yes. Yes, please."

# *13*

*Yes. Yes, please.* Were more beautiful words ever spoken? Garrett longed to crush her to his chest and plunder her sweet mouth. But rushing made no sense. The Brotherhood had been alerted to stay away. He had time, time alone with this amazing women.

Wrapping her in his arms, he lowered his head and savored the pleasure of kissing Anna. Her full lips tempted him beyond reason. He touched down with a groan, fitting his mouth to hers. Magic.

She tucked her warm fingers under his open collar to caress the nape of his neck. His breath hitched. Her light, erotic touch fueled desires he couldn't satisfy. Not now. Maybe not ever.

But he had this—her mouth supple and yielding beneath his. Last night she'd tasted like dreams come true. Still did. So much joy simmered under the surface, waiting to be discovered. He deepened the kiss.

Her hum of pleasure vibrated through him, testing his control. He slid his hands under her parka, impatient with the puffy material in his way. *Just a kiss.*

He skimmed her ribcage and the underside of her breasts as he wound his arms around her. She sucked in a breath.

The brief contact and her quick gasp send a message straight to his groin. If he tightened his grip, she'd find out exactly how she affected him.

Taking his head in both hands, she parted her lips and teased him lightly with her tongue. He answered with some brief forays of his own, his body tightening. His surroundings faded and time narrowed to this moment, this kiss. Anna.

She slackened her jaw, inviting him in. When he plunged his tongue deep, her moan of surrender shattered his restraint. Cupping her bottom, he pulled her close. Now she knew.

Her breath caught. But she didn't back away. Instead she wound her arms around his neck and rose to her tiptoes.

As she wiggled closer, scorching him with every movement of her lush body, the barn door slid open.

He spun so his back was to the door as cold air swept into the barn. He quickly stepped away from Anna as the door closed again. What the hell?

"Damn, I forgot." Matt's voice. "Sorry, bro."

"We can make ourselves scarce, Matt."

A stranger was with him. Wonderful. The guy sounded amused.

"What do you need, Matt?" Sending a glance of apology to Anna, who might never forgive him for this, he turned around. The shock had taken care of his woody, at least.

"I came for a lead rope so I can fetch Thunder." Matt grimaced. "My bad."

"Please don't apologize." Anna stepped up beside him, her head held high. "Garrett kindly invited me to meet some of the horses and have lunch. We got... sidetracked."

Garrett reached for her hand and gave it a squeeze. "This is all on me. I'm the one who—"

"Hey, I screwed up." Matt smiled. "But let's move on. Introductions are in order. Jack, these fine folks are Anna Warren and Garrett Whittaker. Anna's our top-notch receptionist at the Raptors Rise Visitor Center, and Garrett's an excellent wrangler and a damned good mechanic, too."

"Pleased to meet you both." The dark-haired cowboy shook hands with Garrett and tipped his hat towards Anna.

"Jack's from your former stomping grounds, Garrett," Matt said. "He and his family raise Paints at the Last Chance Ranch in Shoshone. Maybe you've heard of—"

"Sure have. Most folks in Jackson Hole know the Last Chance."

"You're from there?" Jack shoved back his hat and studied him. "I thought you looked familiar. What outfit?"

"The Double B."

Jack nodded. "Excellent operation. I haven't been out there in a while, though. Maybe I saw you in Jackson."

"Possibly. How long are you here for, Jack?"

"Just the one night. I'll check out Thunderbolt later." He turned to Matt. "I could use a hamburger and a beer at the Choosy Moose."

"We'll do that, but I advise you to order the apple cider instead of a beer. You'll be glad you did."

"Sounds terrific." He gestured toward the temporary lunch table. "Nice job. We'll leave you to it." He touched the brim of his hat. "Garrett. Ma'am."

Garrett nodded. "Nice meeting you, Jack."

"Be sure and come by Raptors Rise before you go home," Anna said.

Jack sent her a smile. "I'll do that."

As Jack headed for the barn door, Matt held back and lowered his voice. "I'll make it up to you, bro, I promise."

"You don't have to—"

"Yes, I do." He glanced at Anna. "I'm so sorry."

"It's fine."

"We'll talk later." Matt tipped his hat and walked out with Jack.

Garrett waited until Matt closed the barn door before he turned to Anna. "I honestly thought we'd be alone, but that's no excuse. I shouldn't have—"

"Let's talk about it over lunch."

He gazed at her in confusion. "You still want to have lunch with me?"

She chuckled. "I still want to do a lot of things with you, but for now, I'll have to settle for lunch."

He stared at her in stunned silence. Had she just said she wanted... what he wanted? And why wasn't she ripping him a new one for embarrassing her in front of Matt and a visitor?

"Let's have those sandwiches you fixed while we figure this out. Coffee would be nice, too."

"Yes, ma'am. I'll get the cooler out of the tack room." Dazed by her reaction, he managed to fetch the cooler and a large thermos of coffee. She was already perched on one of the tree stumps when he came back.

"I like the seats."

"Henri calls them chummy stumps. Every time we take down a big tree for one reason or another, we replenish the supply of chummy stumps."

"I love it. Great idea."

"Glad you like it." He was waiting for the other shoe to fall as he laid out the meal—turkey sandwiches and potato salad. He put a sandwich on each plate, opened the container of potato salad and stuck a spoon in it. "Take as much as you want."

"A lot." She spooned a generous helping on her plate. "I'm a big fan of potato salad, and I have a hunch you make a good one."

"Folks seem to like it." After taking a seat opposite her, he opened the thermos and poured coffee into her mug. "Should I leave room for cream? I brought some."

"No, thanks. Just fill it up, please."

"Alrighty." He finished pouring hers and took some for himself. After dishing his potato salad, he unfolded his napkin and laid it in his lap. "Ready to talk?"

"In a minute." She picked up half of her sandwich. "But I'd like to dive into this meal, if you don't mind. I'm starving."

"By all means."

She started eating, and between bites she raved about the food. She'd finished half her sandwich and most of her potato salad before she broached the subject at hand. "When Matt first came in and interrupted us, he said *damn, I forgot.* Why did he say that?"

Garrett put down his coffee and sighed. "Because I passed the word to the Brotherhood that we'd be here and I'd rather not be interrupted."

"When did you do that?" She picked up her mug and took a sip of coffee, peeking at him over the rim.

"This morning, after I checked the weather report. Like I said, Jake had already planted the idea in my head." He held her gaze. "I swear all I was going for was a kiss."

"I believe you."

"You do? Even though—"

"Let's face it, Garrett. We're not innocent kids ruled by our hormones."

"I can't claim innocence, but my hormones were definitely in charge a while ago."

"Mine, too. I'm as responsible as you are for where we were headed. Last night you asked me before you kissed me. You did the same thing today. Both times I said yes."

"But you also told me you didn't want to get involved with a guy until Georgie's enrolled in college."

"That was the plan."

"Was?" He held his breath.

"I didn't count on you coming into my life."

"So now what?" His chest tightened.

"I'm not sure." Anxiety clouded her expression. "If I didn't have Georgie, we'd be off to the races, but I have to consider the implications for him."

"We can take it slow, play it by ear."

"That doesn't seem fair to you."

"Let me be the judge of that." He hesitated. "Do you want me to come over for dinner tonight? Or will that be putting too much pressure on—"

"I want to see you, Garrett. I also want Georgie to get used to having you around. Will he? I don't know. And he's still my primary concern."

"Like I said before, he should be."

"Then please come for dinner."

He let out a sigh of relief. He hadn't completely blown it. He still had a shot. "I'll be there."

# 14

Anna convinced Garrett that another kiss would be nothing but trouble, so once they finished lunch, she got in her car and drove back to the visitor center. The snow had stopped except for a few random flurries, so the drive to Raptors Rise was easy.

But the debate going on between her libido and her mothering instincts was hell. Georgie needed a good male role model, a gentle, loving man who would overwrite his early conditioning.

That much of the plan was solid. But she should have found a kindly old gentleman, a grandfather type, not a hot cowboy like Garrett.

That said, she didn't regret one second she'd spent wrapped in his strong arms. When he kissed her as if she were the most precious woman in the world, he healed psychic wounds inflicted by Brad. She needed Garrett as much as Georgie did.

Jake was in the lobby when she arrived. "How was the barn tour?"

"Great." Should she mention that Jake's name had come up? And that Garrett credited him for pointing out a golden opportunity to get her alone? No. She'd let it go except for a report on their visitor, Jack Chance. "Matt came by while we were there. We met Jack."

"I heard about that."

"Word travels fast."

He grinned. "Especially now that we all have mobile phones."

"How much do you know?"

"About Jack Chance?"

"Never mind him. Did you get a report about what went on at the barn during the lunch hour?"

"Not a *detailed* report." His eyes danced with mischief. "Want to give me one?"

"Ummm..." Sometimes she had to remind herself that Jake was her boss. A friend, too, but that didn't mean she could treat him as a casual acquaintance. "I don't think so."

"Fair enough." He looked away, shifted his stance, let out a breath. Eventually he faced her again. "Garrett told me not to talk to you about this."

She couldn't help smiling. "But you're going to, anyway, aren't you?"

"Yes, damn it. I don't want you to suffer through years of deprivation like I did."

"What kind of deprivation?"

"I was starved for love and I wouldn't take a seat at the table."

She blinked. "Oh."

"You look startled."

"I... most guys don't... rather, they're not willing to admit—"

"Exactly. And I was one of those guys. Matter of fact, all of us were, in one way or another.

That's why Henri and Charlie took us in. Every damned one of us were lost souls."

"I didn't know that."

"And you wouldn't know it if somebody didn't tell you. We're not the same men we were."

"I guess not. I wouldn't label any of you lost souls."

"Because we're not anymore. Garrett didn't have the advantage of knowing Charley, but he has Henri and the Brotherhood. He's found his place, his family."

"Then he's a lucky guy."

"And so are we. We think the world of him. So I just wanted to say..." He paused and took a deep breath. "I spent years wanting Millie and not doing anything about it. I knew from the get-go she was the one for me, but I was too scared to go for it."

"You didn't have a kid, though. That changes everything."

"I'm sure it does. But I'd also hate to see you waste years like I did."

She smiled. "I appreciate your concern, Jake. I—" The sound of voices outside the entrance drew her attention. A group of four approached the glass doors. "We have customers."

"We do. That's fine. I could drone on for hours on this topic, but you get the gist."

"I do. You've given me food for thought."

"That was my goal." He grabbed his hat from the desk and set it at a jaunty angle as the doors opened. "Showtime."

\* \* \*

The chili simmered on the stove and Anna was mixing up the batter to make cornbread when her phone pinged with a text from Garrett.

*Can I bring Zeke's daughter Claire to dinner? She wants to meet Georgie. And you.*

Anna typed a quick reply. *I'd love to meet her, too. Find out if she likes chili.*

His answer came in a few seconds. *She loves chili. See you soon.*

Interesting. Why would an eight-year-old be eager to meet a toddler? She'd find out soon enough.

After spooning the cornbread batter into a cast-iron pan that turned out corn-shaped muffins, she stuck the pan in the oven. Then she walked into the living area and pulled the round table a little farther away from the back of the couch.

Squeezing four chairs around it so everyone could see the fireplace was tricky, but since two of the people were children, the arrangement should work. This was assuming Georgie would come out to eat. He'd already voiced his protest of having Garrett over. *Not again, Mama! Don't want Grit!*

The choo-choo noises coming from his room indicated he was currently giving his moose Carl a ride on his wooden train. She went to the doorway. "We have another guest coming for dinner. Her name is Claire."

He glanced up, his expression eager. "Grit stayed home?"

"No, he's coming, too."

"Oh." His body slumped and he glanced at his moose. "Grit again."

"Claire's a little older than you. She just moved to the ranch and she wants to meet you."

"Why?"

"Maybe she's heard what a great boy you are. Maybe she wants to see your room."

"I gots a big room." He ran the train back and forth on the carpet.

"You sure do. Lots of fun stuff in here."

"Grit gots to stay out." He kept his attention on the train.

"He won't come in unless you invite him."

"Good." The rumble of Garrett's truck outside made him scramble to his feet and reach for the door handle. "Gots to close—"

"Wait. If I promise Garrett won't come in your room, will you please leave the door open? For Claire?"

He gazed up at her. "Is she nice?"

"I've never met her. But I've heard she's very nice."

Garrett tapped on the door and Georgie tensed.

"Tell you what. I'll make sure she's nice before I bring her in here. By herself. Without Garrett. How's that?"

He nodded. "Yes, ma'am."

"That's my good boy." She stooped down and gave him a quick hug before going to answer the door.

Garrett met her gaze with a smile that warmed her from her head to her toes. His big hands rested on the narrow shoulders of a blond child dressed exactly like the wranglers at the Buckskin—black Stetson, tooled boots, jeans and a child-sized shearling coat covering what was probably a yoked Western shirt.

The hat shadowed her face but when she looked up, the porch light sparkled in her blue eyes. She stuck out her hand. "Nice to meet you Mrs. Warren. I'm Claire."

Anna shook her hand. "I'm pleased to meet you, Claire. Come on in." She stepped back and motioned them forward. "You can call me Anna if you like."

"Can I call you Aunt Anna?" She peeled off her coat to reveal a blue plaid yoked shirt. "That's what I'm supposed to call the other ladies. Except Gramma Henri, 'cause she told me she's in the gramma age bracket. Which means she gets to buy me things, like this coat."

"I guess I'm in the aunt age bracket, so please call me Aunt Anna. I'd be honored." She glanced at Garrett, who'd closed the door and hung his hat on the coat tree. "Dinner's almost ready, but I haven't started the fire."

He took Claire's coat and slipped out of his own. "I'll do that."

"Can I help you, Uncle Garrett?" Claire handed him her Stetson.

Uncle, huh? She was an aunt and Garrett was an uncle. Cozy.

"You can help me," he said, "but didn't you want to meet Georgie?"

"Oh, *right.*" She said it as if he'd reminded her of the reason for her visit. "Where is he, Aunt Anna?"

"In his room. I'll take you there."

Claire gifted her with a smile. "Okey-dokey."

She glanced at Garrett. "Be right back."

"Looking forward to it."

Awareness flooded her with heat. She'd be smart to douse it. Now they had two children in the house.

As she escorted Claire toward Georgie's room, she called out to him. "I've brought you a new friend, son."

"I saw her, Mama."

Then he'd been spying. That was fine. Curiosity was better than anger or indifference. "Well, here she is." She ushered Claire into his room. "Claire, this is my son Georgie."

He stood ramrod straight in the middle of his room, holding his moose.

"Hi, Georgie." Claire's tone was polite. "Is that a moose?"

He nodded.

"Does your moose have a name?"

He nodded again.

"What is it?"

"Carl."

"Nice name. It has the same letters as mine, only it's missing the *i* and the *e*." Her gaze swept the room and came to rest on his game shelf. "Oh, my gosh, you have Candyland?"

He nodded.

"I used to *love* that game, but I haven't played it in ages. Wanna play it?"

He looked in Anna's direction and she gave him a thumbs-up. He took a quick breath. "Okay."

"Awesome. Is it all right if I get it out?"

Wow. Plenty of adults didn't pay that level of respect to other people's things.

Georgie's posture relaxed. "Sure."

Anna edged toward the door. "I'll call you when dinner's ready."

"Great!" Claire set the box on the floor and opened it. "Thanks, Aunt Anna."

Garrett was crouched on the hearth coaxing the fire to life. He glanced up. "Well?"

"She's amazing."

"You're telling me. This was her idea."

"I don't understand."

"I'll explain." He rose to his feet. "Let's go check on dinner."

"Right."

He wrapped his arm around her shoulders as they headed in that direction. "Missed you."

"Missed you, too." Crazy talk. But she had missed him.

He drew her to a stop in front of the stove. "You didn't leave me much to do."

"I can think of one thing."

"Do we dare?"

"They're playing Candyland."

"That's a game?"

"Yes." Her chest hurt. Who hadn't heard of Candyland? She slid her arms around his neck. "I'm going to kiss you, but not for long. We have to be careful."

He pulled her close. "I'll take what I can get."

Rising to meet him, she zeroed in on his beautifully sculpted mouth and closed her eyes.

The zing of excitement at first contact morphed into the familiar pleasure of his lips moving against hers.

He didn't waste time. The invasion of his tongue tightened her core and sent moisture to all the right places. She fit her body to his, savoring his swift response, the sizzle of desire, the delicious ache that telegraphed the news—that part of her life wasn't dead and gone.

She ended the kiss slowly, easing out of his arms with a sigh of regret. "Sorry, but we—"

"It's okay." He cleared the hoarseness from his throat and dragged in a breath. "I'll just go take a cold shower."

She giggled. "Because that wouldn't be weird."

"Yeah, it would. I'll go roll in a snowbank."

"Please don't."

"Then I only have one trick left." He stepped back and gazed up at the ceiling, his lips moving.

"What are you doing?"

"Running through the parts list for my truck."

"Why are you staring at the ceiling?"

"Because if I look at you, I'll be right back where I started."

"Oh, Garrett. Men have it tough, don't they?"

"I'm not complaining." He took another deep breath and met her gaze. "I'll go through that exercise as often as I'm allowed to kiss you. Because I believe that eventually the time will arrive when I won't have to distract myself."

Her heart beat faster. "It will."

He glanced away. "And... I'm back to inventorying truck parts."

"Would it help to make a salad?"

"Definitely."

"Tomatoes are on the counter, bowl's in the top cupboard in front of you, knives in the drawer to your right." She opened the fridge and pulled out the other ingredients while he rolled back his sleeves and washed his hands at the sink.

Giving him the salad job meant she had nothing to do but watch him. She leaned against the door of the fridge. She could get used to having this man standing at her counter, his wear-softened jeans cupping his tempting backside, his broad shoulders stretching the cotton of his shirt.

If she didn't start making conversation, she was liable to tackle him. "You were going to tell me why Claire is here."

"So I was. She overheard me telling Zeke about Georgie, and next thing I knew, she'd volunteered to be a big sister to him. She thinks she can help, and the fact is, she might be able to."

"I've just met her and I already think she can do whatever she sets her mind to. She's very evolved for eight."

"I haven't had much chance to talk to Zeke without Claire being right there, listening to every word. But judging from what little he's able to say, she had to be mature. Her mother sounds very childish."

"The kind of person who should never have children."

"Right, but Zeke's a great dad, just like you're a great mom. "

"Wouldn't a great mom have addressed Georgie's fears earlier?"

"Like when?" He put down the knife and turned to her. "You've been busy trying to survive, keep food on the table and a roof over your head and Georgie's. You're a fantastic mom."

"Thank you."

"He's not even three yet. There's plenty of time to fix this issue."

"You're right." Plenty of time. *Chill, Anna.* Not an easy task while standing in the kitchen with Garrett Whittaker.

## 15

Garrett had accepted the fact that Georgie's issues meant they had to kiss in secret and hide their budding relationship from that little guy. A full-blown love affair might not happen for a very long time. He hung onto her statement that it would happen eventually.

When dinner was ready, Anna went in to alert the kids while he tended to the fire. In a little while it would be just right for s'mores. Claire would be all for it and Georgie might follow her lead.

Georgie wasn't having dinner with them, though. Anna walked out with Claire but no Georgie.

"I don't get it, Aunt Anna. Uncle Garrett is *wonderful*."

"Yes, he is." Anna sent him a tight smile as she shepherded Claire into the kitchen nook to wash up.

He removed one place setting and took a chair away before heading back to the kitchen nook where Anna was making up a tray for Georgie and Claire was drying her hands. "Thanks for trying,"

"I told him so many good things about you, Uncle Garrett. I said you make the yummiest pancakes and decorate them with chocolate chip smiley faces. I told him you let me help you feed the horses, and that you and Daddy sing to me and we play poker, and—"

"Poker?" Anna's eyebrows lifted.

"I know! Isn't it great? I got to play poker with Daddy, Uncle Garrett, Uncle Rafe, Uncle Jake, Aunt Millie and Aunt Kate. "I won seventy-five cents!"

Garrett waited for his turn at the sink. "It's a quarter buy-in. She's a good player."

"You have to be in this crowd." Claire hung up the towel. "Uncle Rafe calls Aunt Kate a card shark. She's going to teach me some of her techniques so I can be a card shark, too."

"Ever play poker, Anna?" Garrett stepped up to the sink and turned on the water.

"No, and clearly I'm missing out." Anna sounded like she was trying not to laugh.

"You could play with us at the bunkhouse sometime," Claire said. "I could give you a few lessons first, so you'd..." She frowned. "I guess you couldn't bring Georgie, though. He'd freak out."

"Maybe someday." She took a bowl from the stack on the counter and handed it to Claire. "Do you want to serve yourself?"

"I do, but I'm not quite tall enough."

"Here you go." Garrett lifted her up and balanced her on his knee. "How's that?"

"Perfect." She carefully ladled chili into a bowl. "That's enough." She put the ladle back in the pot. "Daddy says my eyes are bigger than my stomach, but I think this is just the right amount so I'll have room for s'mores." She carried her bowl to the table. "Which seat?"

"The middle one," he called out. "So we each get to sit by you."

"And she can be our chaperone," Anna murmured as she picked up Georgie's tray.

"Yes, ma'am. I desperately need one."

"Me, too. I'm totally smitten. I've never had pancakes decorated with chocolate-chip smiley faces."

"The first time I stay for breakfast I'll fix you some."

She held his gaze. "I'd better get out of this hot kitchen." Breaking eye contact, she picked up Georgie's tray. "Would you please dish me some chili?"

"I'm at your command, pretty lady."

"Chili will do it for now." She headed for Georgie's bedroom.

"Hey," Claire called out from the table. "Do you need help with anything, Uncle Garrett?"

"No, ma'am. Everything's under control." Barely.

\* \* \*

Claire kept the conversation going during dinner. She filled them in on her new school, her cool third-grade teacher and the class project that would be launched this month.

"We're gonna build a greenhouse and grow food! Miss Jefferson asked Daddy if he'd help build it and he said sure thing." She pointed to a piece of tomato in her almost empty salad bowl. "I'll bet those tomatoes had to be shipped in."

"Probably," Anna said.

"Our tomatoes will be locally grown." Her eyes gleamed with pride. "Different kinds of lettuce, too. And kale, but I don't know if I like that."

"I like kale," Garrett said.

"I'll bet I'll like it, then. Aunt Anna, did you know Uncle Garrett can cook like nobody's business?"

She chuckled. "I've heard that."

"Uncle Jake can, too. Every Friday night they make his specialty, chuck wagon stew."

"I've heard about that, too."

"Did you know that stew is so good, the cook at the Choosy Moose has begged for the recipe so he can serve it?"

"Nope." She exchanged an amused glance with Garrett.

"But Uncle Jake and Uncle Garrett will never give out that recipe. Uncle Jake said it's a state secret."

"Must be really good stew."

"I wish you could come on Friday night so you could taste it. Oh, wait!" She turned to him. "What if you saved some and brought it to her on Saturday night?"

"I could do that." He looked over at Anna. "If you'd want me to."

"That would be lovely."

"Great." Claire smiled. "That's settled. Friday will be a busy day. We have our Valentine's Day party at school since the actual day is Sunday and Monday is Presidents' Day." She popped the last bit of tomato in her mouth, quickly chewed and swallowed.

"Georgie's daycare is having a little party, too," Anna said. "I promised to make some heart-shaped cookies."

And what was he doing for Anna for Valentine's Day? He hadn't given it a single thought, and that was unacceptable.

"Aunt Lucy's going to help me decorate my shoebox." Claire's face glowed with excitement. "She's a good artist. I got my Valentines today from Aunt Fiona at Planet-Friendly Paper. She has *so* many Valentine's Day cards in there!"

"I'm sure she does." He should pay a visit to Fiona's shop. He needed way more than a card, though. He needed a plan.

Claire finished off her chili and peered at his bowl. Then she checked out Anna's. "Can we have s'mores, now?"

"We sure can." Anna pushed back her chair. "While we're clearing the table, would you please let Georgie know we're getting ready to make them?"

"Yes, ma'am!" Claire was out of her seat like a shot.

Garrett helped Anna carry everything to the kitchen nook and load the dishwasher. "Think she'll get him out here?"

"I don't know. She couldn't do it before." She took the s'mores fixings out of the cupboard.

"By the way, I could bring the stew over Friday night so it's fresh out of the pot."

She shook her head. "That's sweet of you, but to hear Jake tell it, Fridays are about socializing with the Buckskin gang, too."

"They are, but the Brotherhood's decided to gather at the bunkhouse tomorrow night, so I'll get my dose of togetherness then. If I skip coming over here Friday night, too, we'll miss another chance to work on Georgie's problem."

She smiled. "And another chance to see each other?"

"That too, but I—"

"It's okay, Garrett. I want to spend time with you. I'd love you to bring the stew over fresh out of the pot."

"Excellent." His gaze lingered on her full mouth. He craved another taste, but it was too risky.

"The Brotherhood decided to meet before Valentine's Day to gather advice on navigating the holiday?" She sounded tickled about it.

"Yes, and since you've brought it up, I'd like us to do something special Sunday night. But I don't—"

"We can't make it a romantic evening with Georgie here. That would cause trouble."

"I could fix dinner for you, at least. Maybe get a bottle of champagne."

"I don't know. Giving me special treatment could set him off. Brad used to act lovey-dovey when he wanted to pull my attention away from Georgie. I'd resist and he'd start yelling and throwing things. I think Georgie remembers that progression, at least on some level."

His gut tightened. What a bastard.

Anna laid a hand on his arm. "I'm sorry, Garrett. It's jacked up. Don't worry about Valentine's Day. Let it go."

He swallowed a growl of frustration. "I'll think of something. It's a special day and you deserve—"

"So do you." She gave his arm a squeeze. "I'd like to do something nice for you, but the situation makes that tricky."

"Do you take him to daycare on Sundays?"

She shook her head. "Sunday and Friday are my days off, so normally he doesn't go those days. I'm taking him in Friday afternoon because Erica wanted to have a little Valentine party for the kids and I didn't want him to miss it."

"With dancing?" That video of Georgie two-stepping had stayed with him.

"I'm sure. I'll have my camera phone at the ready."

"Since you're off on Friday, what do you think of taking him down to the barn in the morning? I could find out if Lucky will be around, or Prince."

"He'd probably like that. I try to do special things for him when I have time off. That would be an adventure for him, and now I know how nice the horses are."

"Good deal. I'll check the schedule. If Lucky isn't assigned to a trail ride, that would be perfect."

"Aunt Anna?" Claire sounded like she was still in Georgie's room. "Could you please come here a minute?"

"I'll be right there."

"I'll get the fire ready and the s'mores set up."

"Thanks." She hurried off to Georgie's room.

He carried the crackers, marshmallows and chocolate over to the fire, found the small folding table she used and set everything up. The fire had burned down until it was a perfect layer of glowing coals. He unhooked the toasting forks from their place near the fireplace and laid them across the table.

When Anna came out alone, he figured Georgie had refused once again.

She walked closer and lowered her voice. "He's wearing his Spiderman costume. Carl's mom gave it to me and it was tight on him in October, so it's splitting at the seams. But he thinks you won't recognize him in the suit. And bonus, he has superpowers."

"He's right. He's the most powerful person in this cabin."

Her gaze locked with his. "Does that bother you?"

"Yes. But I'm not jealous, if that's what you're worried about."

Her silence confirmed that she was.

"I am angry, though. Your ex did a number on you and Georgie. Because of that, both of you are suffering. I hate seeing that."

"You can bail anytime."

"No way. That would be worse." He picked up a fork. "We're making s'mores."

## 16

The glint of steel in Garrett's eyes had startled Anna. The gentle soul she'd come to care for in the past few days had temporarily transformed into a warrior. If Brad had been standing in front of him, her abusive ex would be sprawled on the ground, recovering from a right to the jaw delivered by her avenging angel.

But Garrett had doused the flames of battle the second Claire had come out leading a three-foot version of Spiderman wearing his ill-fitting and faded Spidey suit and his cowboy hat.

Moving away from the fireplace, Garrett stayed nearby and waited until she got Claire and Georgie started.

Georgie asked Claire to help him hold the toasting fork, bypassing his mother. Claire's efficient movements proved that she was perfectly capable of handling the job. After a slight prick of jealousy, Anna let out a sigh of relief. Time to sit back and let someone else nurture her kid.

Claire monitored Georgie with a kindness and selflessness far beyond her years. Surely she wanted to make s'mores as much as he did, but she postponed her turn until she'd helped him make one. Then she patiently supervised while he moved the mask away from his mouth so he could savor his treat.

In less than two hours, she'd forged a solid bond with him. She was a natural at it, solicitous and a little bossy. Georgie followed Claire's instructions more carefully than he'd ever followed hers. Who knew he'd desperately needed a big sister?

She was so absorbed in the interaction that when Garrett held out a warm s'more, she blinked in surprise. "You made this for me?"

"I did. Snuck over here once I figured the kids wouldn't notice me."

She glanced in Claire and Georgie's direction and sure enough, they weren't paying any attention to the grownups. "Is it burned?"

"No, it's carefully curated, toasted gently on all sides, just like you prefer."

"Thank you."

"Are you going to eat it?"

She met his gaze. "I'm letting it cool down so it won't burn my tongue."

"Good idea. I'd hate for you to burn your tongue. I've grown fond of it."

His soft-spoken words and the teasing light in his eyes sent a ripple of arousal straight to her core. "Watch yourself, buster."

"What did I say?" He widened his eyes, innocence personified.

"You know perfectly well what you said. That's a charged subject."

He lowered his voice another notch. "Everything's a charged subject where you're concerned."

"Not my fault."

"Not mine either. Eat your s'more, okay? It's best when it's hot."

"Uh-huh." His outrageous flirting was having a predictable effect on her, one she couldn't do a darned thing about.

Might as well eat her s'more. She bit into it and encountered a sweet explosion of creamy marshmallow and soft chocolate. Only one sensual treat compared with this, and it involved kissing a certain cowboy.

She chewed slowly, savoring the mixture of tastes and textures. Eventually she swallowed. "Best s'more ever."

"Yeah?" He smiled. "I wasn't sure I could do it to suit you since I'm used to the flame method. It's really good?"

"Very good. You should take the time to make one like that for yourself. I guarantee once you taste it, you'll change your method."

"All right. Challenge accepted." He skewered a fresh marshmallow, crouched by the fire and began slowly rotating the fork over the hot coals.

After checking on the kids, who were doing just fine without her, she settled back on the couch to finish her s'more and indulge in some covert Garrett watching. Probably a bad idea, because the more she looked, the more she wanted him.

"Mama." Georgie stood by her knee. His voice was muffled by the Spidey mask, but an undercurrent of tension came through. "Don't want Grit, Mama."

Claire appeared behind him. "I'm sorry, Aunt Anna. I told him not to worry about Uncle Garrett, but he—"

"He gots to go home." Georgie crawled up on her lap. He was shaking. "Please, Mama."

She wrapped him in her arms. Had he picked up on the flirty mood between her and Garrett? "Okay, son. We'll call it a night."

Garrett stood. Clearly he'd heard the exchange. Pulling his partially toasted marshmallow off the fork, he set it on a saucer. "I'll get our coats, Claire."

Georgie scrambled off her lap. "Claire doesn't gots to go!"

"Yes, I do, Georgie." She leaned down and gave him a hug. "My daddy's waiting for me at home."

"You gots a *daddy*?"

"A wonderful one. I love him very much."

"What about your mama? Do you gots a mama?"

"Yes, but I don't live with her, now. I live with my daddy."

"Where?"

"In the bunkhouse. Uncle Garrett lives there, too. It's the funnest place I've ever lived." She looked toward the door where Garrett stood waiting, her coat and hat in his hand. "Well, gotta go, Georgie. I'll see you again soon, okay?"

Georgie sniffed.

"Don't cry. I'll be back. We'll play Candyland again." She walked toward the door.

He started to follow her and hesitated. Then, with a sob, he ran to his room and shut the door.

Anna walked over to the front door, her gaze fixed on Garrett. "I'm so sorry. I thought we were getting somewhere."

"We were. We are."

"You think so?"

"Definitely. He just came to the end of his rope. But for a while there, he forgot to be scared of me." He helped Claire on with her coat. "You were awesome, sweetheart. This was a terrific idea."

"Thanks." Before she put her hat on, she gave Anna a hug around the waist. "I had a great time. Good chili, too. And of course I *love* s'mores."

"Did you get enough?"

"Yes, ma'am."

"I hope so. I appreciate all the effort you put in tonight. I just wish—"

"We'll get there, Anna." Garrett's tone was gentle. "This is a time that calls for slow toasting."

She managed a smile. "Right."

"Slow toasting?" Claire looked confused. "What's that got to do with anything?"

"Uncle Garrett's reminding me to be patient."

"Oh. Like with the marshmallows. I get it." She sighed. "Poor Georgie. He could have so much fun on this ranch if he'd just let himself." She opened the door. "Beat you to the truck, Uncle Garrett!" She took off at a run.

Garrett started after her, but then he came back, pulled Anna close and gave her a quick kiss.

"Hang in there." Then he turned away, hurried across the porch and jogged to the truck.

Anna watched him go as cold air chilled her kiss-moistened lips. He'd said he wouldn't kiss her in front of Georgie, but he'd had no problem kissing her when Claire was likely watching. What would that wise little girl have to say about that?

# <u>17</u>

"Uncle Garrett, are you in love with Aunt Anna?"

He gulped and started the truck. "That's a big question."

"If you want my opinion, I'd say you are."

"Why do you think so?"

"I see you watching her when she doesn't know you're doing it. That's how a man looks when he's in love."

"How do you know how a man looks when he's in love?"

"Well, duh. Movies."

"Ah."

"Uncle Jake thinks so, too. He talked about it while we were playing poker, before you got there."

"I see."

"He thinks you and Aunt Anna would be great together. That was another reason I asked to come with you tonight, so I could meet her. Uncle Jake's right. You're perfect for each other."

He started laughing. "How old are you?"

"Eight, but that doesn't mean I don't know things."

"I'm sure you know a lot of things, but you just met me a few days ago. That doesn't give you much to go on."

"That's what you think. Don't forget I live in the bunkhouse with you. I know you're neat, and so is she. You care about other people. She does, too. You're polite and you listen. Aunt Anna's like that."

"So we're both nice people. That doesn't mean we're meant for each other."

"Maybe not, but there's a good chance you are. And you're already to the kissing stage."

"You saw that, huh?"

"Of course. I beat you to the truck because you went back so you could kiss her. And it wasn't a first kiss, either."

"How could you tell?"

"You rushed it."

"Good grief. I didn't know I was living with a private investigator."

"I've thought of being one, but I've never heard of a private investigator who's also a wrangler."

"There's a first time for everything."

"I guess so." She stopped talking.

With some kids, moments of silence meant they'd run out of things to say. He doubted that ever happened with Claire. Chances were excellent she was thinking.

She took a deep breath. "Uncle Garrett, you need help."

"I'm sure I do, but you'll have to be more specific."

"I tried my best, but my best might not be good enough. It's time to call in Gramma Henri."

* * *

"I think consulting Henri is a great idea." Matt leaned his wheelbarrow against the back wall of the barn and took off his gloves. "You look surprised."

"I am surprised." Garrett had been paired with Matt for barn duty. While they'd fed the horses their breakfast, he'd convinced Matt the interrupted kiss was no big deal. He had far greater problems. "I only told you Claire's comment to make you laugh. I don't know what Henri could do about this."

"I don't, either, but she's a smart lady."

"She is, but I've been here less than a year. The rest of you might be comfortable discussing your love life with her, but I'm not."

"So don't. Ask her for suggestions regarding Georgie."

"She'll figure out why I'm asking. I'd rather throw this out to the Brotherhood tonight during our sleepover."

"We can do that, too. And come to think of it, Henri will be busy today getting ready for the Babe's blowout. She might not have time to sit and chat, anyway."

"Right. I'm not dismissing the idea of talking to her, I just—"

"Want to put it off?"

"Yeah, like forever. The Brotherhood will probably come up with some great suggestions."

"Maybe, but it could be helpful to get a woman's point-of-view, especially when it comes to kids, and I... hang on. Brilliant idea incoming." Matt shoved back his hat and smiled. "Yep, that's it. Sometimes I amaze myself."

"You want me to talk to Lucy? Talking to her would be less intimidating for me, if that's what you're getting at."

"You will end up talking to her if this plan works, but I'm thinking bigger. Much bigger." Matt chuckled. "We've never done anything quite like this, but it makes perfect sense to combine forces if they'll go for it. I think they will."

"Who?"

"The Babes. The Brotherhood will schedule a joint session with the Babes around the fire pit tonight."

"You're kidding, right?"

"No sir. If the Babes and the Brotherhood can't come up with answers to this issue, I'll eat my hat."

"I just told you I don't feel comfortable talking to Henri about this and you want to bring in the Babes?"

"The Babes plus Ellie Mae Stockton. She's driving up from Eagles Nest. That woman—"

"Forget it, Matt. It's a terrible idea."

"It's not a terrible idea. I get why you'd rather not have a private talk with Henri. This'll be way easier, more relaxed. Drinks will be flowing and it's mostly dark so you can't see expressions as well. I'm telling you, it's an elegant solution."

"The Babes might not want to."

"Like I said, I think they will. Trust me, bro, you'll be thrilled with the way this turns out."

"Do I have veto power?"

"No. This problem goes beyond you. It involves you, but it's really about that little boy."

Garrett chewed on that for a while. "You're right. I'll be there."

"Good man." Matt gave his shoulder a squeeze. Then he glanced toward the open barn door. "Hey, Jack! Excellent timing. Come on down."

Garrett glanced at Matt. "He hasn't seen Thunder yet?"

"Oh, no, we came back later. Looks like we'll be doing some business."

"That's great, Matt. Glad to hear it." He turned toward their visitor. "Good to see you again, Jack." His info about the Chance brothers was coming back to him. Jack was half Shoshone, which explained the prominent cheekbones. His dark hair was streaked with gray, but the guy didn't have an ounce of fat on him.

"Same here." Jack extended his hand. "I hope things worked out with Anna."

"It's… complicated."

"Been there. Things smoothed out after Josie and I took that walk down the aisle, though." He grinned. "Although we haven't hit the teen years, yet."

"Good-looking family," Matt said. "Jack showed us pictures last night during dinner."

"Because that's what I do, foist pictures of my kids on everybody, whether they want to see them or not." He pulled out his phone. "Want to see my kids, Garrett?"

"Absolutely."

"While you're doing that," Matt said, "I'll call Lucy and tell her we're on our way over for breakfast." He walked a short distance down the barn aisle before making his call.

"So this is Archie, my oldest, during a junior cutting horse competition. That's Warrior, his pride and joy."

"Looks like they both know what they're doing."

"They do. Won that day." He lowered his voice. "Jake filled me in on your situation. You're probably getting advice coming at you from every direction."

"Not so much yet, but it looks like I'll be getting a truckload of it very soon."

"Well, here's mine. Hang in there. Kids are resilient. I have a feeling things will work out."

"That's encouraging."

"Lucy's put the coffee on." Matt tucked his phone in his pocket as he walked back toward them. "I told her we'd start over in a few minutes. Thought you'd want to snap a few more shots of Thunder before we leave."

"Sure do."

"And I'd better get going," Garrett said. "It's Claire's first day of school. I want to give her a hug before she leaves."

Jack glanced at him. "Your daughter?"

"She's my... niece." He was still getting used to that.

"Well, then, nice meeting you, Garrett." Jack held out his hand. "I'm heading home today, but I'll be back. I'll probably bring Josie, maybe the kids."

"Great. I look forward to it."

"If you ever need anything, you know where to find me."

"Thank you." He tipped his hat and hurried out of the barn with a lighter heart. Jack Chance, one of the most respected men in Jackson Hole, had a feeling things would work out. Maybe he was right.

# 18

As Anna packed up the remains of her lunch in preparation for leaving the small kitchen/breakroom and going back to work, Millie walked in.

"Jake told me you were on your lunch break."

"Just getting ready to go back out there. What's up?"

"Kate and I are keeping Claire tonight, so we decided to invite Isabel and the baby to stay over. Would you and Georgie like to come spend the night with us? Kate and Rafe's cottage has three bedrooms, so there's a fair amount of room. I think we can make it work."

"Georgie would be ecstatic to see Claire. He calls her Sissy, which I figure she taught him. He can't stop talking about her."

Millie laughed. "Nobody can stop talking about her. We didn't know we needed a Claire at the Buckskin, but clearly we did. Then you'll come?"

"I will and thank you. What can I bring?"

"Don't worry about food. Kate and I will handle that. Isabel's making her awesome coffee from Cup of Cheer for our breakfast."

"I'd like to contribute something."

"An adult beverage?"

"I have two six-packs of apple cider. I'll bring that."

"Excellent. And a few things for Georgie to play with would be a good idea. That should do it. Come over around six. Claire and I'll be there, and probably Isabel and Cleo Marie. Kate will show up when she's finished at the dining hall. This will be so much fun!"

"It will." Anna beamed at her. "I haven't been to a slumber party in ages."

"Then it's about time. Speaking of time, I need to run. Got some errands in town."

"I'll walk out with you so Jake can get some lunch. You guys could grab a meal in town."

"He packed himself a sandwich because he knows I'm shopping for his Valentine's present today."

"I see. Then I guess—" She lost her train of thought. Garrett was in the lobby in deep conversation with Jake.

"Look at those two. They must be solving the world's problems judging from the looks on their faces." Millie said it loud enough to be heard across the room.

Jake stopped talking and smiled at her. "Heading into town?"

"I am."

"Gonna buy me that snow blower?"

"I'm getting you something way more romantic."

"A snow blower's romantic. Less shoveling, more time for mattress bingo."

"I want that in writing. See you all later." Millie sailed out the front door with a wave of her hand.

A family with two small girls wearing matching parkas approached the entrance and Anna glanced at Jake. "I've got this."

"I'll take care of them." Jake walked toward the desk. "Garrett wants to talk to you about something."

"Oh?"

"You two can go back to my office."

"Okay." Where was Jake's conspiratorial wink? Or his sly grin? Instead his expression remained serious. "Is something wrong?"

"Not at all. I just want to give you some privacy."

"Thanks, bro." Garrett gestured for Anna to go ahead of him down the hall.

She stepped into Jake's office. His desk was cluttered and he'd left his computer on—typical Jake mode, always in the middle of doing something. He'd hung several of Lucy's framed sketches on the wall and packed his bookshelf with reference books. She'd read several of them since coming to work here.

Garrett closed the door. "In case you're wondering, he didn't shoo us in here so we could make out."

"Why did he, then?" She turned to face him.

"I want to fill you in on what's happening before you hear it from someone else."

"Is it something bad?"

"No. Just unusual." He took off his hat and laid it on top of the papers on Jake's desk before moving in her direction. "If I start kissing you I'll forget all about this other thing, but I could use a hug."

"Me, too." She craved his touch, but maybe she'd better keep that to herself. Moving into his arms was more natural than breathing.

He drew her close, his gaze locking with hers. "God, you feel good."

"You, too."

"Are you spending the night with Kate and Millie? Jake said they were going to ask you."

"I am. It's kind of them. Georgie will be so excited."

"His perfect scenario. No big scary men."

"And he'll get to see Claire. He's asked me a thousand times when she's coming over again. She made a conquest."

"She's made a bunch of them." He massaged her back. "But that's not what I want to talk about. Like I told you before, these Brotherhood gatherings are often used to come up with solutions to a problem one of us is having."

"Such as Valentine's Day plans?"

"That. And this issue with Georgie."

"Georgie? Really?"

"Yes. I thought you should know. This is how the Buckskin gang tends to tackle things, as a group."

"Did you ask them to discuss this?"

"Not in so many words, but they all know I'm looking for ways to help him get over his distrust of men."

"Huh. I suppose it can't hurt to toss around some thoughts, but Zeke's the only one with first-hand experience raising a kid. CJ's barely into the process."

"True." His palm drew lazy circles over her back. "That's why Matt's invited the Babes to join in the discussion."

She stared at him. "Tonight? Isn't the sleepover a brothers-only deal?"

"Normally, but Matt figures they'll add a woman's perspective and they'll already be gathered at Henri's. Makes sense for them to come over for a couple of hours."

"Have they done this before when you were brainstorming a problem?"

"I don't think so."

"Why now?"

He shrugged. "Because it's convenient?"

"If only I could hear what they have to say firsthand. Would I be allowed?"

"Of course."

"Never mind. I can't leave Georgie in a house he's never been to with people he barely knows, even for an hour or two. That's not fair to anyone."

"But he's okay with daycare."

"Because I introduced him to it gradually. And he already knew Carl. His mom and I used to trade off babysitting until her boyfriend moved in. Then Georgie refused to go over there anymore."

"I'll tell you everything I can remember when we get a chance to talk again."

"I appreciate that." She snuggled closer and gazed up at him. "I guess Georgie and I are considered part of the group, after all. You told me that on the day of the accident, but I didn't quite believe it. I'm beginning to, though."

"Good." He stroked the line of her jaw with his thumb. "Now that I've delivered my message, I don't have an excuse to stay here with you."

Her heartrate picked up. "That's too bad."

"I know. Seems a shame to waste this opportunity, though." He cupped her cheek. "Just one kiss?"

She smiled. "I've heard that before."

"And you'll be hearing it every time I can steal a few minutes to do this." As his lips touched down, he caressed the corner of her mouth with his thumb, coaxing her to slacken her jaw.

The sweet invasion of his tongue stirred a longing deep in her core. She pressed against him, wanting... more.

He groaned and thrust deeper as he pulled her in tight. She trembled in the grip of a fierce ache, a powerful need that stole her breath. She squirmed closer.

He lifted his head, his breathing harsh. "Anna... when you do that..."

She swallowed and forced herself to back away. "You're right." She gulped in air and met his heavy-lidded gaze. "I'm urging you on and that's not fair. I wanted your kiss. I want... everything. Which is crazy." She dragged in another breath. "We're in no position to—"

"I'll bet we could find one." He held her gaze. "This office is filled with possibilities."

"And we won't explore any of them."

He sighed. "No, we won't." He gave her a crooked smile. "But that doesn't stop me from thinking about it."

"Or me."

"One day I will make love to you, Anna."

She took a deep breath and straightened her clothes. "But not today."

# <u>19</u>

The Brotherhood launched into full party mode that night, with Garrett and Jake cooking a feast worthy of royalty. And why not? The Babes were coming.

For the first time since Garrett had hired on at the Buckskin, the Babes were including a visit to the bunkhouse as part of their monthly blowout routine. They'd been down here a couple of times in the past year for special events like Rafe and Kate's wedding reception, but never on the spur of the moment.

"This combined gathering feels unusual." Garrett unwrapped a package of steaks. "Is it?"

"It's only happened once before." Jake ladled a spicy sauce he'd created over a large dish of grilled chicken. "They came when Charlie died, after Henri had spent the day handling the details of that. I'm not sure who was supposed to be comforting who, but we needed to be together, just us. We all got stinkin' drunk."

"Makes sense."

"That was a sucky time." CJ stood beside him chopping veggies. "Be glad you weren't here."

"Matter of fact, wish I had been. I would have loved to know him."

"Wasn't the same as now, though," Jake said. "Seth was here and he's in Eagles Nest. We didn't even know about Zeke back then, and Matt had given up on ever seeing Lucy again."

"And now Lucy's a member of the Babes," CJ said. "Lucy and Matt will be the only married ones here."

"Hey, I'm married." Jake tucked the chicken dish in the oven. "Finally."

"So am I," CJ said. "That's not what I meant. Millie and Isabel aren't here. They're—"

"I know. Just pulling your chain. Where is Zeke, anyway?"

"He put himself in charge of the fire," Garrett said. "Since Henri's the only Babe he's met, I think he's a little intimidated that they're descending all at once."

"I didn't think of that." Jake fell silent for a moment. "Maybe I should've—aw, hell, too late, now. Hey, Garrett, are the steaks ready to take out to the fire pit?"

"Just adding seasoning to the last filet." Nice to see Jake's protective nature kicking in. "But like I said, I have limited experience cooking over an open fire."

"You'll do fine. You have good instincts."

"For cooking. But when it comes to Anna..."

"Bro." CJ waved a carrot in his direction. "Don't be putting yourself down. You're the one who advised me to scatter rose petals on the bed when I was trying to impress Isabel. Not sure you can find any this time of year, but you could talk to Beth at Racy Lace. She might even have fake ones."

"I can manage okay when I have room to maneuver, but this situation has me hog-tied."

"And that's one of the things we hope to accomplish tonight." Jake lifted the lid on a pot of simmering wild rice. "Loosen up those knots."

"Jake, we've got us an emergency." Rafe stormed into the kitchen. "We don't have enough cider for a group this big." He turned as Matt came through the kitchen door. "Matt, did you know we're low on booze?"

"I did, and I—"

"The market's closed." Rafe plowed on. "I might be able to talk Ben out of a case or two. Unfortunately, that requires a trip to the Moose, and we don't have enough time to—"

"We're covered, Rafe. Sorry, it's been a long day and I forgot to tell anybody. Ed's bringing her pricey champagne. She promised we'd have enough to make us all very happy."

Rafe grinned. "Well, then. Problem solved. But Kate's gonna be jealous as hell if she finds out we were drinking Ed's champagne tonight. She loves that stuff."

"Well, you're in luck, because Ed asked if she should bring extra bottles for members of the Brotherhood to take home to their sweethearts for Valentine's Day, and I told her that would be very much appreciated."

CJ sighed. "Ed's the best. Well, not *the best*. Henri's the best. We all know that. But Ed—"

"Her party food is awesome," Rafe said. "All those different stations for every kind of food you can imagine. I pig out every time we go there for a barrel racing demonstration."

"Let's face it." Nick walked in on the tail end of the conversation. "When Ed sets out a buffet, she does it right. And her chef makes the best desserts in the world. Is she bringing any of those little chocolate cupcakes?"

Garrett glanced at Jake. "Are you feeling somewhat unappreciated right now?"

"I do believe I am. Maybe we should go relax out by the fire pit with a cool one and let these morons finish up. CJ can tell them what to do."

"Sounds good." Garrett abandoned his tray of filets and walked to the fridge. "Rafe said we're low, but I'm wagering we can find a couple of bottles to soothe our battered egos."

"Okay, okay." Matt stepped in, waving both arms. "Let's give Jake and Garrett some love. They've cooked more meals for our sorry asses than Ed's chef ever did. And with less resources. If we let them walk off the job and the food for the Babes isn't up to par, that's on us."

Much groveling followed, and Garrett worked very hard not to laugh. But Matt had a point. Ed had the resources to make a splash with very little effort on her part. The Brotherhood could approach that standard, but they had to bust their buns to do it. He, for one, liked the challenge.

"They're here." Leo made the announcement from the bunkroom where he was fooling with his sound system. CJ would play some tunes to start because that had become a tradition. Then Leo's system would provide music for the rest of the evening.

"We should go out." Garrett wasn't sure where that idea came from, but it sounded right. "We'll escort them around the house instead of making them go through the kitchen to get to the fire pit."

Matt nodded. "When you're right, you're right. Each of you take a Babe. Leo, you're with Ed. CJ, you've got Anastasia. I mean *Red*. Nick, you're with Pam. Jake, you're with Lucy."

"You're not taking Lucy? She's your wife!"

"That's why I'm escorting Peggy. We need to mix it up. Rafe, you take Josette. Garrett, you're escorting Henri."

"Henri? But I'm the newest one here. I shouldn't be—"

"All the more reason you should do it. That leaves us with Ellie Mae Stockton."

Zeke came through the kitchen door. "What's going on?"

"The Babes just pulled up, bro," Jake said.

"Ah." His shoulders tensed.

"I'm assigning who escorts who," Matt said. "We're left with Ellie Mae from Eagles Nest, who's not technically a Babe."

"Well, I'm not technically a member of the Brotherhood, so let me escort Ellie Mae. Where am I taking her?"

"Around the house and back to the fire pit. Garrett suggested that would be classier than parading them through the kitchen."

"Agreed."

Matt gazed at him. "A word of warning. She's eighty-something and she likes younger men. You might be just her cup of tea."

Zeke's shoulders came down a notch and he smiled. "Can't wait to meet her."

Grabbing his coat and hat, Garrett headed out the front door. Escorting Henri was an honor. He wouldn't have chosen it considering his status as the new hire. Compared to the years his brothers had worked at the Buckskin, his time was nothing.

But Matt had the authority. With Seth gone, Matt was the most senior of the Brotherhood members. If Matt wanted him to escort Henri to the fire pit, he'd jolly well do it.

Pairing up Babes and members of the Brotherhood turned out to be relatively easy with Matt in charge. The Babes grasped the concept and cooperated.

Ellie Mae greeted Zeke with an *oo-la-la* loud enough for everyone to hear. "You must be new. I would have remembered such a handsome cutie-pie."

"That's Ellie Mae for you," Henri said as she took Garrett's arm. She lowered her voice. "I'm glad Matt called us in. We had a preliminary discussion about the situation before driving down here."

"I appreciate the effort you're all making."

"It's what we do. When I drove Anna and Georgie to daycare the other day, she filled me in on Georgie's problem, so the Babes are all up to speed on that, and your plan to spend time with him."

"I think it might work, but it's likely to take a while."

"That's what Matt said. And in the meantime, you and Anna can't enjoy each other."

He'd turned up his collar against a chilly breeze. Big mistake. He needed that cold air to neutralize the heat rising from his neck to his face.

"I've embarrassed you."

"Yes, ma'am, a little bit."

"I apologize, but this problem is important, too, and clearly it won't solve itself, either. Matt said he and Jack interrupted a hot kiss."

"Yes, ma'am."

"Can I assume Anna would like to have some time alone with you?"

"I—" He cleared his throat. "I believe she would."

"That's good information, Garrett. Or should I call you Grit?"

He laughed, and some of the tension eased from his chest. "I'm kinda proud of that nickname."

"It suits you. You know, when little kids give you a nickname, they usually end up calling you that for years, maybe even when you're old and gray."

"I could live with that." Especially if it meant he'd be turning old and gray with Anna.

## 20

When Anna pulled up in front of Kate and Rafe's cottage, lights glowed from the windows and smoke drifted from the chimney. She parked beside Millie's truck.

She'd barely had time to unlock the doors and climb out before a blond whirling dervish hurtled across the porch, her coat half on.

"You're here!" Claire grabbed her around the waist and squeezed. "Aunt Anna, can I help you get Georgie out? I want to see how those car seats work."

"Sure thing. I—"

"Mama! Out, Mama!" Georgie bounced in his seat. "Sissy, Mama!"

"I'm coming, Georgie! Sissy's here!"

"You taught him that, right?" Anna rounded the front of the car to get to the passenger side.

"Yes, because he was having trouble saying my name. I love being Sissy. I wanted a baby brother so bad when I was younger."

That explained a lot. By the time Anna opened the back door, Georgie had turned his request into a chant of *out-Mama-out-Mama* as he rocked back and forth in his seat. She showed Claire how to release Georgie, who was beside himself with joy.

"Can I lift him out?"

"He weighs thirty-one pounds. Have you ever picked up anything that heavy?"

She hesitated, tapping her finger against her chin. "Maybe you'd better do it."

"Good decision."

"Grit getted me out," Georgie muttered.

"Yes, he did." She lifted him from the seat and lowered him to the ground. "He saved us from the snowbank. He's a hero, like Spiderman."

"No." He clutched his moose to his chest.

She gripped him by the shoulders and crouched in front of him. "No, what?"

He gazed at her steadily. "No, don't want Grit." He tried to wiggle away.

She held on tighter. "No, *ma'am.*"

"No, ma'am."

"Okay. Now you can go in with Sissy."

"Okay!" He raced over to where she stood waiting. "Sissy, we gots Candyland!"

"Where?"

"Right here." Anna pulled the board game from the floor of the passenger seat, where she'd tucked it so it would be easily accessible.

Claire hurried over. "I can carry it in for you."

"Thanks."

Taking the game, she stepped closer, her voice soft. "I think it's great that you make him mind his manners."

She smiled. "I'm guessing your daddy did the same when you were little."

"Yes, ma'am.

"Sissy, we gots to play Candyland!" Georgie tugged on her jacket.

She turned to him. "We will. And guess what else? Aunt Millie found her game of Chutes and Ladders." Wrapping an arm around his shoulders, she walked him up the steps. "I used to play that one, too. It's fun. Hey, I see you brought Carl!"

"Yep."

Anna picked up a tightly packed duffle from the front seat and slung it over her shoulder. Then she popped the trunk and walked back to get Georgie's Spiderman sleeping bag.

"Can I help?" Millie came down the porch steps tugging on her jacket, her copper-colored hair loose around her shoulders. "I heard you drive up but I was in the middle of chopping onions for lasagna."

"Yum. I love lasagna."

"What can I carry?"

"The two six-packs are on the floor of the back seat, if you want to grab those."

"Will do." She opened the back door and pulled out the cartons. "Thanks for bringing these."

"Will it be enough?"

"Plenty. We have some in the fridge and Isabel brought over her virgin brew since she's nursing." She started back toward the house.

Anna fell into step beside her. "Claire gave us a warm welcome."

"I knew she would." Millie climbed the steps and Anna followed.

"We put you and the kids in my old room, first one on the left as you go down the hall." She tucked one six-pack under her arm and opened the door with her free hand. They're already in there playing Candyland."

"They didn't want to set it up out by the fire?"

"I suggested that, but they chose the floor of the bedroom. Claire asked if we had a card table and a spare sheet to make a tent. I promised to round that up for her."

"A *tent*. Georgie's gonna be in heaven." Anna walked into the cozy living room. "Wow, Isabel, you and Cleo Marie look like a picture out of *Parenting* magazine sitting by the fire in the rocker." Isabel's dark eyes and dark hair, cut in a short, asymmetrical bob, were compliments of her Portuguese ancestors. Her daughter, at least for now, had fuzzy blond hair and blue eyes, CJ's coloring.

"She loves watching the flames. How are you? I keep thinking I'll get over to the visitor center to say hi, but I never seem to make it."

"You have a baby to take care of and a coffee shop to run. I can't imagine when you'd have spare time to run over to the visitor center for a chat."

"Evidently I don't, so I was excited to find out you were coming. Go put your stuff down and we'll get this party started."

"Alrighty!" How long since she'd had a girls' night? Very long. She walked quickly toward the hall and made a sharp left into the first bedroom.

Georgie glanced at her, eyes shining. "Mama, I winned!"

"Almost," Claire said. "I still have a chance."

"I gots a *bigger* chance." He focused on the board.

"Looks like you guys are all set, then." Anna put the duffle in a corner, laid the rolled sleeping bag on the bed and unzipped her parka. "Georgie, I brought in your sleeping bag." And she'd forgotten something. What? Oh, yeah, she'd left her purse in the car.

He looked up again. "Sissy's makin' a *tent*, Mama."

"I heard that."

"We're sleepin' in it. Carl, too."

"I brought the card table." Millie came through the door, a card table in one hand and a blanket in the other. "Where do you want it?"

Claire stood. "The far corner, please."

"You bet." Millie handed her the blanket. "I brought this instead of a sheet. It won't slide as much."

"That's perfect, Aunt Millie."

"If the table's in the corner, that will help hold it, too." Millie stepped around the board game as she carried the table to the far corner of the room and unfolded the legs.

Georgie scrambled up. "Let's maked the tent, Sissy!"

"Don't you want to finish our game?"

"No, let's maked the tent!" The second Millie put it down, he crawled under it.

"Okay." Claire shrugged. "The tent it is." She gazed at Anna and Millie with a tolerant smile. "He's easily distracted."

Anna laughed. "I've noticed."

"Need anything else?" Millie surveyed the room.

"Snacks!" Georgie called out.

"Say *please*, son."

"Snacks, please."

"I'll bring you some crackers and cheese." Millie met Anna's gaze and tipped her head toward the hallway. "Happy Hour time."

"Lead the way." She hadn't seen Georgie this animated in ages. "Claire is a gem," she said once they were out of earshot.

"She's an amazing little girl. The woman who gave up custody of that child must be a wacko."

"Her loss is our gain. Listen, I forgot to bring my purse in from the car. I'll be right back."

Cold air made her shiver as she left the warmth of the cottage to retrieve her purse. After she took it from the front seat, habit made her pull out her phone and check for messages. She had a text from Garrett.

*Thinking of you. The Babes have arrived. I'm testing my outdoor barbequing skills. He'd included a picture of the fire pit with steaks on a grill suspended over it.*

The message warmed her from her head to her toes and certain places in between. He was surrounded by his favorite peeps, busy with cooking chores, and yet he was thinking of her. And texting her to let her know that.

She texted back. *Looks delicious.*

His reply was instant. *If it turns out I'm good at this, we can try it in your fireplace.*

Clearly he missed her and wanted to keep the connection going even though they were apart. She was in the same boat. She typed *I'm game!*

*Excellent. Have fun with Kate, Millie and Isabel.*

*I will. Good luck with the discussion.*

*I'll let you know how it goes.*

She started to type a reply and paused. She was standing in the cold sending texts like a teenager because he'd reached out and she didn't want to break the connection.

Texting him a thumbs-up emoji, she silenced her phone and tucked it back in her purse. Time for girls' night.

## *21*

Ed's pricey champagne went down so easy that Garrett lost track of how much he'd had. With cider, he could count bottles, but when he kept the same glass and someone was always refilling it, how could he gauge his intake?

Good thing he was sitting on a chummy stump that forced him to maintain his posture. Lounging in an Adirondack chair, he might get completely sloshed. Those chairs had gone to the Babes, who could hold their liquor better than any man he knew, including him.

However much bubbly he'd consumed, he had a slight buzz going. Just as well. It would help him deal with an upcoming discussion that would horrify him if he had to handle it stone-cold sober.

They'd already covered Georgie's situation and had come up with some ideas for transforming him into a pint-sized cowboy.

The plan had promise, especially since Claire, the person Georgie idolized, loved cowboys. Surely he'd want to belong to the tribe Claire held in such high-esteem.

But as Henri introduced the next topic, he topped off his bubbly and drained his glass. They were about to discuss his sex life. Or lack of it.

"Let me be clear," Henri said. "Garrett hates the idea of talking about this. He's very old-school. He's convinced that men should work through this kind of issue on their own."

Jake smiled. "So how's that going for you, bro? "

"I've made progress."

"If we're talking about stealing a few kisses here and there," Matt said, "that's scant progress."

"It's only been a few days. And Anna and I don't want to upset Georgie. I'm trying to earn his trust, not scare him more."

"We all respect that." Red, who'd decided to rename herself to match the color of her hair, raised her champagne glass. "Here's to nobly considering the wishes of others."

Pam reached over and tapped her glass to Red's. "I'll drink to that."

Peggy giggled. "Me, too, but then I'll drink to anything tonight. I didn't check the year on this batch, Ed, but I'll bet it's a good one."

"It is, but we're not here to discuss the quality of the booze. The way I see it, two responsible adults are delaying sexual gratification to avoid traumatizing a toddler. Is that the gist?"

"Sounds more noble when you put it that way," Rafe said. "But there still ought to be a way around that barrier."

Garrett rolled the stem of his glass between his palms. "Look, I'm not sure I want a way around it. Georgie's—"

"Are you serious?" CJ held out his flute as Jake came around with a freshly opened bottle. "In your shoes, I'd be searching high and low to find a way to distract that little shaver so you can make love to his sweet mama."

"Nope." Garrett shook his head. "Her ex used to try to seduce her to draw her attention away from Georgie. I don't want to do anything that would remind her of him."

"I don't see her presenting you with solutions, bro." Jake poured Garrett more champagne. "It's not in her nature to go looking for a babysitter so she can make whoopee."

"You're right," Garrett said. "She doesn't like asking for help, especially when it comes to Georgie. I had to talk her into asking Henri for a ride into town so Georgie could get to daycare. I'm telling you, this is a complicated—"

"No, it's not." Ellie Mae sat forward in her chair. "It's simple. Make love to each other if you both want to. Use condoms if you're fertile and you don't want bambinos. That's my formula. It's worked for years."

Ed rolled her eyes. "Tell me about it."

Garrett couldn't help smiling. "You're forgetting about Georgie."

"No, I'm not. He's too little to understand. He doesn't have to know a thing about it until he's ready for the information."

"He'll know if I'm in his house. Which he does think of as *his* house. He doesn't want me there for dinner, let alone spending the night."

Red finished off her champagne. "I'm getting a vibe of guilt feelings from Anna that would louse up Ellie Mae's perfect formula."

Josette groaned. "Guilt. *C'est terrible.*"

"I'm giving up guilt for Lent this year," Pam said. "That puppy's a killer."

"I couldn't agree more," Henri said. "That's why we need to present Anna with an opportunity for guilt-free sex with Garrett."

He choked on his champagne.

"Easy there, bro." Jake came over and slapped him on the back. "Man up. You can get through this."

He wasn't so sure. His coughing fit lasted an embarrassingly long time. Tears blurred his vision as he glanced around the semi-circle. Every single person was grinning.

Jake squeezed his shoulder. "First time on the hot seat is the toughest."

"No kidding." He cleared his throat and took a breath before he turned to Henri. Maybe the dim light would keep her from seeing how much he was blushing. "How do you propose to do that, ma'am?"

She gave him a warm smile of approval. "I thought you'd never ask."

\* \* \*

"You both need to relax your shoulders." Millie came over and gently pushed Anna's shoulders down and moved on to Isabel's. "You can't do a decent shimmy if your shoulders are tight."

All three kids were asleep with their bedroom doors shut. Millie and Kate had decided to teach Anna and Isabel the shoulder shimmy for the gang's next trip to the Moose.

Anna doubted she'd be going anytime soon, but she'd always wanted to learn this. She rolled her shoulders and held out her arms as Millie turned on the music, a tune by Luke Bryan called *Country Girl.* She wasn't a country girl yet, but she was living on a ranch, drinking hard cider from the bottle and kissing a handsome cowboy every so often. That was a start.

The two teachers faced their pair of students as the fire crackled in the background.

"Start slow and build up to it." Kate demonstrated the technique again. "One shoulder forward, then switch. Back and forth, back and forth."

"Keep your hips still and facing forward." Millie moved to the beat like a pro.

Anna struggled with the unfamiliar movement.

"Smile ladies," Kate said. "Have fun with it."

Fun. There was a concept. Anna blew out a breath, rolled her shoulders and tried again, this time with a smile.

"Better." Millie nodded. "Now pick up the pace."

Anna swiveled her ribcage and moved her shoulders faster. "This is a workout!"

"You know it." Kate grinned. "But worth sweating for. I can bring Rafe to his knees with this move."

Anna laughed. "The power of the shimmy."

"Woo-hoo!" Isabel tossed her head. "Girls, I'm feeling *sexy*. Look out, CJ. Your hot baby-mama's got it going on."

"Preach it, sister!" Millie began singing along with Luke Bryan.

When Kate and Isabel joined in, Anna did, too, breathlessly, because the shimmy was way harder than it looked.

What a blast, though. She'd left her girlfriends in Indiana and hadn't made new ones here. Brad had discouraged it and then she'd become a single mom with no extra time for socializing.

Millie had said these overnights were a regular thing. Millie, Kate and Isabel had been welcoming and friendly. She'd be invited back. Cool.

Millie stopped singing. "Is someone at the door? I thought I heard knocking."

"Yeah," Kate said. "There it is again. Cut the music. I'll go see who it is." Breathing hard, she walked to the door and opened it partway. "Oh, hi. Want to come in?"

"Better not."

Anna sucked in a breath. *Garrett*?

Kate opened the door wider and stepped back as cold air swept into the living room. "Come on in. Georgie's fast asleep, if that's what you're worried about."

"I was, but—" His gaze locked with Anna's as he stepped inside and Kate closed the door. "I didn't mean to interrupt. I just wanted a moment with Anna."

"To report on the discussion?" Heart beating like crazy, she walked toward his gorgeous self. The shimmy practice had heated her blood and his sudden appearance turned it up several notches more.

"Yes, ma'am."

"You two can go in the kitchen," Kate said. "That's if you want some privacy."

"I appreciate that." He took off his hat and ran his fingers through his hair. "But Georgie might wake up and want a drink of water or something. I think it'd be better if Anna comes out to my truck."

"Oh, he won't wake up," Anna said. "We've been out here dancing and singing. Haven't heard a peep from the kids."

"But that could always change." Millie gave her a look that she couldn't quite read. "You should play it safe like Garrett says and have the conversation in his truck."

Kate nodded. "Definitely. Don't take chances." Then she ducked her head. A tiny snort of laughter gave her away.

Anna got the message. Garrett was asking for some private time and they were urging her to take advantage of the opportunity. "I'll grab my parka."

Garrett helped her on with it and ushered her out the door. Muffled laughter followed them. He chuckled. "I guess they think we're going to make out."

"Aren't we?" She shivered as cold air hit her still sweaty body.

"The thought crossed my mind." He wrapped an arm around her shoulders as they descended the steps.

Okay, not cold anymore. Shivering for a different reason.

"But I honestly did come over to relay information and give you a chance to think about it." He started to open the front passenger door and paused. "We can talk better in the back."

She started laughing. "Talk better? It's way more cramped than the—"

"I know, but—"

"Never mind. Let's get in the back and *talk*."

"We're not having sex back here." He opened the door and the dome light came on as he helped her in.

"Good, because at least one of us would dislocate something."

He climbed in, sat down and closed the door. Then he turned to her. "When we make love, we're going to do it right."

Her breath caught. The dome light was still on, allowing her to see his expression. Something had changed. "You sound confident that will happen."

"I am, now that the Babes have come up with a plan."

Her heart beat in triple time. "Are we talking about how to handle the issue with Georgie or—"

"Everything. Georgie, you, me." He took a deep breath, his gaze intense. "Us."

# 22

"Us?" Anna's eyes widened. "But there is no—"

"Oh, yes, ma'am." Tossing his hat in the front seat, he drew her close. "There most certainly is." The dome light flicked out, but he didn't need it for this. He captured her mouth, sinking into the wonder of kissing Anna.

She moaned and kissed him back, fumbling with the buttons of his coat, sliding her hands inside, eager for this, eager for him.

He kissed her thoroughly, stoking the fire. No us? Who was she kidding? Their passion was more real than the ground under their feet, the sky sprinkled with stars above their heads.

Tasting her lips was heaven, but it wasn't enough. He nuzzled her jaw and the curve of her throat, unzipped her parka and slipped his hand under her shirt to unfasten her bra. His blood racing, he cupped her warm, silken breast.

She gasped and arched into his caress.

"Don't tell me there's no us." His voice rasped in the stillness. "Your heart's going a mile-a-minute." He brushed his thumb over her taut nipple.

"So's yours." She pressed her hand against his chest.

"Because I want you. And you want me."

Her breath hitched. "But we can't."

"Yes, we can." He squeezed gently as he returned to her mouth and placed light kisses there. "Not tonight, but soon."

She pulled back. "How?"

The front porch light barely reached to the truck, but it was enough for him to tell she was looking at him. "Georgie's needs are important. I'm not minimizing that fact at all. But ours are, too."

"What... what are you saying?"

"Henri's offered to keep Georgie and Claire the next time the gang goes out for dinner and dancing at the Moose. Red volunteered to stay at Henri's and help, too."

"When?"

"This Saturday."

She sucked in air. "Day after tomorrow?"

"Too soon?" He drew her back into his arms and combed his fingers through her hair. "What do you say, Anna? Will you come dancing with me?"

"Then what?"

"If Henri's place works for Georgie, he'll stay there. And I'll spend the night with you."

She tensed. "That's a big step."

"But is it a step you want to take?"

"We talked about waiting until Georgie gets used to you."

"Which we could still do. However, I got a different perspective tonight and I'm considering it. I'm hoping you will, too."

She was quiet for a moment. "Can you give me some time?"

"Sure can. All the time you need."

She took another deep breath. "Did you discuss Georgie? Or just this?"

"We discussed Georgie first. Henri would like to escort you and Georgie to the barn tomorrow morning at eleven if you're still okay with going. She'll make sure Lucky Ducky's in residence and the rest of us are elsewhere."

"That would be great."

"You can text her when you go back inside."

"I will."

"And Ed wants to buy Georgie a pair of boots."

"Oh, wait. That's not—"

"Hear me out. Ed's hoping you'll agree to come into town with Henri for lunch and then you can all go boot shopping for Georgie."

"That's sweet of Ed, but I don't want her to waste her money, either. I've heard she has a ton of it, but that's doesn't mean she should spend it on boots for a little kid who'll outgrow them lickity-split."

"Then you can donate them to charity. Or save them for Cleo Marie."

"I hadn't thought of passing them down. But still...."

"The boots are part of the strategy. The more he identifies with cowboys, the more likely he'll warm to the ones on the ranch, specifically, me. Oh, and by the way, Claire has boots. Claire's another part of the strategy. She loves cowboys. And what Claire loves—"

"Georgie might start loving. It could work. Okay, I'll go along with the boots idea, but I'll pay for—"

"Anna." He hugged her closer. "I get your reluctance. Been there. Took me months to understand that the Babes live for opportunities like this. They treasure their status as honorary aunties for the Brotherhood. They love to spoil us rotten."

"I'm not a member of the Brotherhood and neither is Georgie."

"But you're very important to a member of the Brotherhood, which makes you and Georgie very important to the Babes."

She lifted her face to his. "Seems like they're playing matchmaker."

"I suppose they are."

"Are you fine with that?"

"Yes, ma'am. But just remember this—the ball will always be in your court."

"In that case, could I have one more kiss before I go inside?"

"Yes, ma'am." He kissed her with all the longing in his heart. Then he reluctantly let her go. To his immense surprise and joy, she came back for more. He gave her more, and the heat built until his fly pinched and his breathing grew ragged.

He broke away again. "I have to stop. Either that or shove some snow down my pants."

Her short laugh was breathy and strained. "I might need to do the same." She stroked his cheek. "I do want you, Garrett. I'm just afraid I'll start something I can't finish."

"No worries. I'll make sure you do."

"That wasn't what I meant and you know it."

"Thought I did, but I decided to clarify in case you had doubts about that issue."

"My doubts lie elsewhere." Reaching under her shirt, she fastened her bra.

"Okay, then. One more thing." He cupped her face in both hands. "I want you with the heat of a thousand suns, but that's not all there is to it."

"I know that." She placed her hands over his. "That's where my doubts lie."

"Hey, I'm tougher than I look."

"No, you're not." She gave him one more quick kiss. "Now you'd better let me out before Millie, Kate and Isabel send a search party."

He reached for the door handle. "Brace yourself. It's cold out there."

"That's okay. I'm tougher than I look, too."

"No, you're not." He opened the door and helped her down. "I'll walk you to the door."

"No, don't. I'll just run in. Get back in that truck, cowboy." She turned and started toward the cottage.

He went after her. "Dammit, Anna." He caught her by the arm. "I can't just let you go off like that. It's not right."

"You have to leave or I'm liable to kiss you again."

He swept her into his arms. "Like that's a bad thing." His mouth came down on hers and the cold air meant nothing because he was kissing Anna and she was a furnace.

At last she broke away, gasping. "See what happens?"

"Yeah." He grinned. "And I like it."

## 23

Getting teased by her three new friends was fun. None of her Indianapolis friends had teased her about Brad. They hadn't liked him. Why hadn't she paid attention to that?

After Millie, Isabel and Kate wound down a little, she revealed the proposed plan for Saturday night. They were all for it.

"I don't know. It's like I'm colluding with Georgie's enemy."

"Except he's a friend," Millie said. "Georgie just doesn't know that yet. But eventually he will."

"This makes me think of something that came up over the holidays." Isabel put down her bottle of virgin cider. "When my folks were here, my mom noticed that CJ and I were focusing entirely on our baby and starting to ignore each other."

"You're lucky CJ pays attention to Cleo Marie. Brad couldn't be bothered with Georgie."

Millie spoke up. "Which was an excellent reason to leave him, but..." She hesitated. "Never mind. I'm probably overstepping."

"No, you're not. I could use some advice."

"Well, you don't have a husband to ignore, but Isabel makes a good point. Maybe you're ignoring yourself."

The words hit home. "Garrett said something similar, that Georgie has needs, but... so do we."

"That's tough to remember when you're a mom, though." Isabel reached over and squeezed her arm. "This Saturday night deal has me thinking, too. I'm not ready to leave Cleo Marie overnight, but with Henri and Red on duty, maybe I could leave her for a couple of hours. And show off my shimmy."

"Hey, Anna." Kate turned to her, a gleam in her blue eyes. "You can show off your shimmy, too. Make your teachers proud."

"I'll admit I've already thought of that. I haven't danced in so long. Until tonight, I'd forgotten how much I love it."

"Then it's settled," Millie said. "You're going with us to the Moose Saturday night."

"What if I just plan to do that and forget about the rest?" Her question stirred up a chorus of objections.

"You can't send poor Garrett home to sleep in the bunkhouse," Kate said. "That's not cool."

"Yeah, okay, you're right. But here's the issue. I'm miles away from making a commitment. I think he's inches away. Am I being fair to him?"

"Ask him." Kate took a swig from her cider. "I guarantee he'll tell you he doesn't care. He's too far gone to be worried about whether this experiment will crash and burn. Sleep with the guy and put him out of his misery."

Anna started laughing. "An act of mercy?"

"Absolutely!" Kate grinned. "He's been interested in you ever since Leo described your spunky attitude during Operation Santa."

"Oh, I'm sure. The oblivious mom who let her child kick Leo in the nuts."

"No," Millie said. "The sweet mom in dire circumstances who touchingly still wanted a picture of her son with Santa Claus. Jake cracked up when Leo told the story, but then he took another look at your situation and got serious about the idea of hiring you. I'm so glad he did."

"Me, too." She took a drink of her cider. "I love working at the sanctuary. And living in that adorable cabin. And meeting you guys."

"And meeting Garrett." Kate gave her a sly look. "Don't tell me you're not thrilled about that, because I know better."

"Yes, I am."

Millie gazed at her. "So you'll say yes to the entire plan?"

"I will." Not surprisingly, all three women cheered. She waited until they'd finished toasting her decision before turning to Millie. "I've been wanting to ask this ever since I got here. Would you give me your version of the flaming hoops story?"

"Be glad to." She smiled. "But I'll open with a commercial. The members of the Brotherhood are special. If you have a chance to become involved with one, don't hesitate."

Anna met her gaze. "Message received."

* * *

The relaxed evening was followed by a breakfast that was served crazy early. Fueled by Kate's egg casserole paired with Isabel's fresh-ground coffee, a fruit plate and sweet rolls, the women scattered in different directions.

Kate left to cook for the ranch guests and Millie had cabins to clean. Isabel drove into town to open Cup of Cheer with Cleo Marie in tow. Claire got ready for school and Millie gave her a ride to the bus stop.

As the only one with the day off, Anna offered to stay and straighten up the cottage. Georgie followed her around while she worked. She gave him as many tasks as he could handle and fielded questions about Claire's whereabouts and when he'd see her again.

She kept her answers simple. Claire was in school and he would see her in two days. When he wanted more details, she switched the subject to their upcoming trip to the barn. Focusing her attention on Saturday night created a firestorm of sensations in her body and destroyed her ability to accomplish anything.

And she had a busy day. Although Kate had told her not to spend any time cleaning the cottage, she wanted to leave it tidy. Kate and Millie had fed her two meals and offered a big dose of female friendship. She was grateful.

Back in the cabin, she baked the Valentine's cookies for the daycare party and rushed through a shower for her and a bath for Georgie. She'd texted Henri this morning to make sure they were still on for the barn visit. Kate had mentioned that the Babes sometimes partied until dawn.

If they had this time, Henri gave no indication. She promised to be there at eleven, and sure enough, her tan truck was parked in front of the barn. It was the only vehicle in sight.

"Miss Henri's here, Georgie."

"I wanna see Miss 'enri, Mama."

"And you want to see the horse, Lucky Ducky, too, right?"

"Yep! He goes *huh-huh-huh*."

She grinned. During his bath, he'd asked what sound a horse made. Instead of attempting the whinny she'd heard in movies but never personally experienced, she'd mimicked Lucky's low-throated chuckle. Georgie's version was cute as hell.

When she pulled up on the driver's side, Henri opened her door, climbed out and gave her a wave. Then she leaned down and tapped on the window next to Georgie's car seat.

"Miss 'enri, Mama! Miss 'enri!"

"I know, sweetie." She popped the locks and got out. "The door's open if you want to spring him from his seat."

"You bet I do." Henri opened the door. "Georgie! How're you doing, cowboy?"

"I gots my hat." He tugged it down over his snowsuit hood.

"I see that. Looks great on you."

Anna rounded the car and paused as Georgie pointed to Henri's Stetson.

"You gots a hat, too."

"Just like yours."

"Yep. Sissy gots a hat."

Henri looked confused.

"That's Claire," Anna said.

"Oh." Henri smiled.

"Grit gots a hat."

Anna held her breath. Would he follow that with his usual negative statement?

"Because he's a cowboy," Henri said with a quick glance at Anna.

"Yep."

When he didn't add *don't want Grit,* Anna let out a sigh of relief. It was a small victory, but a victory nevertheless.

Henri leaned into the car. "Let's get you out of there, okay?"

"Okay!"

She lifted Georgie out of his seat and balanced him on her hip. Thirty-one pounds of toddler was no problem for this lady.

"Miss 'enri?"

"What, Georgie?"

He took a quick breath, his expression earnest. "Lucky Ducky goes *huh-huh-huh.*"

"Yes, he does! How'd you know that?"

"Mama tolded me."

"Well done, Mama." Henri winked at her. "Let's go see that sweet horse, shall we?"

"Okay!"

"I can carry him, Henri."

"I'm fine. It's not every day I get to do this. You can open the door for us, though."

"Absolutely." She hurried forward and pushed the door open. It was heavier than it looked.

Good thing she'd been lifting a toddler on a regular basis. "Thanks for coming."

"I wouldn't miss this for the world. The party broke up earlier than usual since I had this barn visit scheduled and Ed's meeting us for lunch in town."

"I haven't said anything to him about that part." She followed Henri and Georgie into the barn. "I thought we'd better see—"

Georgie gasped as he caught sight of Lucky poking his head over the stall door. "Mama," he said in a stage whisper. "*Look.*" Eyes wide, he pointed toward the horse.

"I see him, son. Isn't he beautiful?"

Georgie nodded, riveted by the large animal staring at him.

Henri moved forward slowly. "Georgie, I'd like you to meet Lucky Ducky." She used the same gentle tone Garrett had when talking to the horses. "Lucky, this is Georgie. You're the first horse he's ever met. Can you say hello?"

Lucky bobbed his head and made the low chuckling noise Anna had heard before, the one she'd taught Georgie this morning.

"Mama, he said it." Her son quivered with delight. "He goed huh-huh-huh."

Over the crown of Georgie's hat, she met Henri's gaze. They exchanged smiles. Although she itched to grab her phone and capture his awestruck expression, she might ruin the moment. Not worth it.

Henri shifted him to her other hip. "Would you like to touch Lucky's nose?"

"Yes, ma'am."

Anna's heart melted at the note of reverence in his voice. She'd been worried that he'd be afraid. Instead he was acting as if he'd been given a rare privilege.

Henri walked up to the stall, reached out and lightly stroked Lucky's nose. "Do it like this." She positioned him so he could easily reach.

Leaning closer, Georgie copied Henri's movement. Then he did it again and smiled. "He likes it."

"I'm sure he does. He's very fond of children."

Then Lucky snorted.

Georgie jumped, and Anna pressed a hand to her chest. Would that scare him? Would he make a fuss and want to leave?

Instead he giggled and pointed at the horse. "He sneezed, Mama! He goed *a-choo!*"

"So he did, son." She relaxed. He was awed, but not the least bit afraid. How ironic. A big horse didn't scare him at all. But an adult male sent him running for cover.

## 24

"Have you heard from Anna?" Jake dished three servings of stew into an insulated container while Garrett packaged up coleslaw and hot rolls.

"Not yet."

"Ah."

"Henri texted me, though. The visit to the barn was a hit and Georgie was excited about his new boots. Anna had a lot going on today." And she might still be thinking.

On the other hand, she might have made her decision after talking it over with Millie, Kate and Isabel after he'd left. Even if she hadn't, Millie would likely have filled Jake in on what was discussed. He snapped the lid on the coleslaw container. "Did Millie say anything about last night?"

When Jake didn't reply, he asked again. "I figure there was a discussion after Anna went back in the cottage. Did Millie mention anything to you today?"

After screwing the lid on the container, Jake tucked it in the canvas bag on the counter.

"She did, didn't she?"

Jake faced him, his expression apologetic. "Yes, but she made me swear not to—"

"Damn it, Jake! I need to know what—"

"I can't tell you. She made me promise. I shouldn't have asked if you'd heard from Anna. I thought by now she would've contacted you."

"You're killing me, bro. Can't you give me a hint?"

"No. It's Anna's to say. Millie... oh, God, here she comes."

Millie sailed through the back door of the kitchen. "Claire asked if she can serve the stew. I told her—Jake, why are you looking guilty?" Then she sucked in a breath. "Please tell me you didn't—"

"He hasn't said anything." Garrett turned to her, his heart on fire. "But have mercy! At least give me some indication—"

"It's not my place, much as I'd love to." She came over and hugged him. "Sorry." She gestured toward the canvas bag. "I suggest you take off. This will be Anna's first taste of chuck wagon stew. You don't want to serve it to her cold."

"No, ma'am." He grabbed the bag, fetched his coat and hat and barreled out the front door. On the drive over to Anna's cabin, he made himself drag in several deep breaths. He couldn't go racing in there thinking she'd blurt out her answer.

She might not even have one. Maybe she was waiting to see how Georgie reacted to his presence when Claire wasn't around to run interference. The Babes could talk all they wanted about the right to indulge in adult activities. They weren't the sole caretaker of a toddler.

Smoke drifted from the chimney when he pulled up to the cabin. He was a little later than usual because he'd waited until the stew was done. Made sense that she'd gone ahead and built a fire.

Yeah, he liked doing that for her, bringing in wood, tending the fire so it would end up a perfect bed of coals for s'mores. Would that be on the menu tonight?

He switched off the engine. Would they have precious moments alone or would Georgie return to his spying routine? Anything was possible with that little guy.

And with Anna, too. She might go the entire evening and not mention the plan for tomorrow night. He'd told her she could think about it. He'd put the ball firmly in her court.

*Nice job, doofus.* With those parameters, he couldn't even ask her about it. Climbing out, he walked around to the passenger door to fetch the canvas sack from the floor of the cab.

Would Georgie like chuck wagon stew? It was on the spicy side. So far Anna had planned their dinner menu, probably around things Georgie would eat.

A little face appeared at the window, nose pressed against the glass. Then the face was gone. He sighed. Arriving with Claire had been easier.

But she'd been incandescent with joy at the prospect of tonight's gathering of the Brotherhood and their sweethearts. She'd be the belle of the ball and that made him smile. He'd soldier on without her.

Anna opened the door as he climbed the porch steps. "Georgie's been keeping an eye out for you."

"So he can dash into his room?" He drank in the sight of her. Many long hours had passed since he'd held her in his arms. He ached to do it again.

"He did that, but..." She stepped back to let him in. "He seems less panicked about you coming this time."

"Really?" He was afraid to put too much faith in it. "Does he know Claire's not with me?" He walked in and glanced toward Georgie's room. No sign of him. The table had been set for three.

"He knows she didn't come this time." She closed the door and turned toward him. "I explained that she's at the bunkhouse with her daddy. I said they're eating the same stew you're bringing to us. He seemed to like that idea."

Handing over the bag, he hung his hat on the coat tree. "Everyone said to tell you hello. They all hope you'll—" Nope, couldn't mention that, either. "They hope you'll enjoy the chuck wagon stew." He took off his coat.

"That isn't what you were going to say." She moved closer.

"No." He put his coat on a hook. "Forgot myself for a minute."

She took one more step toward him and lowered her voice. "The answer is yes, I'd love to go dancing with the gang tomorrow night."

His heart beat so fast he was lightheaded. "Great! They'll be excited." And? He took a deep breath. Maybe he should just be happy that she'd agreed to that much, but—

"I also told Georgie he'll see Claire again when they spend the night at Miss Henri's house."

He closed his eyes as the breath whooshed out of his lungs. "Thank you."

"I decided last night, but I didn't have time to call. It didn't seem like the sort of thing to put in a text."

He opened his eyes and met her gaze. "I would have taken that info any way I could get it. Text, email, walkie-talkie, carrier pigeon..."

"I should have texted last night. I just... wanted to tell you in person."

"I get it. I do. And right now, I want to kiss you so bad and I don't dare."

"Yeah, better not. If we're making progress, and I think we are, we'd be foolish to take chances." She stepped out of kissing range and held up the bag. "Let's get started. I'm hungry." She headed for the kitchen nook.

"Care to be more specific? Some of us might take that as a suggestive remark."

She laughed. "Some of us have sex on the brain."

"Some of us can't help it when contemplating future events."

"Now I'm thinking I should have told you at the end of the evening instead of the beginning. You'll be in a state the whole time you're here."

"Like you won't?"

She reached the kitchen and set the bag on the counter. "I've been in a state ever since you left last night." She turned, her dark eyes gleaming.

"And if we know what's good for us, we'll change the subject."

He clenched his fists to keep from reaching for her. "Right." Clearing his throat, he glanced at the floor and did his best to quench the fire raging in his veins. When he'd partially succeeded, he looked up again. "You set three places at the table. Do you think he'll eat dinner with us?"

"No, but he's already asked about s'mores. And he put on his Spiderman suit."

"With his Stetson?" Concentrating on Georgie helped.

"And his boots. Spidey's gone country."

"Whatever it takes."

## 25

Georgie asked to eat in his room and Anna let him if he kept the door open. She took his food in while Garrett delivered their meal to the table behind the couch and brought a bottle of cider for each of them.

When she came back, he pulled out her chair for her. "I saw Georgie's Valentine on the fridge. Great job."

"It is. He had some help, but Erica said he drew the picture by himself." She glanced up as he scooted her in. "Thanks. Cowboy courtliness is fun."

"It's fun for me, too. Gives me a great excuse to lean down and do this." He gave her a light kiss.

"Careful." Her lips tingled. "You could start a fire."

"I plan to. Tomorrow night." He took his seat next to her.

"I thought we agreed to change the subject."

"That was kitchen rules. We're in the living room, now. New location, new rules." He put his napkin in his lap.

"How do you figure?"

"We have to be more careful in the kitchen. We could forget ourselves. It's happened in there before."

"I remember." She shivered at the prospect of endless kissing... and more. Taking a breath to steady herself, she ate a spoonful of warm stew. Delicious.

"Out here, we're more in the public eye. Certain people could appear at any moment." He dug into his meal, too.

"So true. Certain superheroes." She took another bite.

"So what I just did won't happen again. I got away with it once, but I won't risk it a second time."

"Good plan." The stew was amazing. Although it didn't replace what she wanted, it was a halfway decent substitute and eating it kept her mouth occupied.

"But we can still talk about it." He continued to eat.

"We'll just frustrate ourselves. Let's discuss something else." She alternated with bites of coleslaw and rolls, also excellent.

"Like what? My mind is full of the topic you don't want to talk about."

"Then don't talk at all. Eat your food and drink your cider. This meal's terrific. I had no idea what I was missing every Friday night."

"I'll make sure you get stew every week from now on."

They ate in silence punctuated with the crackling of the fire. Or maybe not complete silence.

Eating without talking was erotic when the man next to her would be her lover tomorrow night.

The lips he pressed to the neck of his cider bottle would be busy elsewhere. The arm that brushed hers would be wrapped around her naked body. The hand that grasped a salad fork would be...

Her breath hitched. "We need to talk."

"We do?" He sent her a concerned glance. "Are you reconsidering your—"

"No, no, I didn't mean *we need to talk* like we have an unresolved issue. I mean not talking during this meal lets me think about what will be happening in a little more than twenty-four hours."

He lowered his voice. "Getting a little hot under the... um... collar?"

She glanced at him. He was smiling, the rat. "Yes, I am. I suppose you're cool as a cucumber."

He grinned. "My cucumber is the opposite of cool. I'm grateful for the generous cut of your napkins."

"*Garrett.*" She grabbed hers and ducked her head as she did her best to muffle her laughter.

"Just telling it like it is. And by the way, your time estimate has us leaving the Moose immediately after dinner. Do you really want to eat and run? I'm fine with that, but I—"

"No, I don't want to eat and run, for goodness sakes." She glanced up. "How would that look?"

"Doesn't matter to me how it looks." His eyes gleamed with mischief. "We can skip the Moose completely if you'd rather grab takeout and come straight back here."

"Absolutely not."

"You're sure? Because I don't want to keep you waiting if you're that—"

"Stop it." She couldn't help giggling. "You're terrible."

"You don't know that, yet. And FYI, I'm bringing my A-game."

She gulped. "We need a distraction ASAP."

"Got one?" The amusement faded as his gaze darkened to navy. "Because I'm fresh out."

"Um..." She was caught, ensnared by the heat in his eyes.

"Stop looking at me that way, Anna."

"Then you stop looking at me like that."

"I can't help it. I just want—"

"Mama! All done, Mama!"

She dragged in a breath and pushed back her chair. "Be right there, son." Her distraction had arrived. She had one for Garrett, too.

Hurrying to the coat tree, she reached in her purse and brought her phone back to the table. Garrett was already on his feet, clearing the dishes.

She tapped the phone and handed it to him. "I have a video of Georgie dancing at the Valentine's party today. Should've thought of that before we sat down. It would have solved our problem."

He caught her wrist before she could leave. "It's not a problem." His voice was warm, his gaze even warmer. "It's a gift." Bringing her hand to his mouth, he kissed it. Then he smiled and let her go.

She floated into Georgie's room buoyed by his heartfelt words, romantic gesture and tender smile. Millie's words echoed in her head. *The*

*members of the Brotherhood are special. If you have*
*a chance to become involved with one, don't hesitate.*

\* \* \*

The prospect of s'mores convinced Georgie to suit up and come out of his room. Anna helped him put on his Spiderman mask and settled the Stetson over it. He tugged on his boots by himself, a bonus that had been a selling point from the moment he'd tried them on in the store.

"Gots boots, Mama." He stomped a few times to emphasize the point.

She longed to take a picture of this getup, but kindness stopped her. And the fact that Garrett had her phone. "Ready to go out by the fire?"

His small chest heaved. "Yep."

"Take your food tray with you and carry it to the kitchen."

"Yes, ma'am."

"You're a brave boy, Georgie."

"Yep."

He was very brave. A grown man represented a dragon to him, yet he was going out there to face the beast and enjoy his s'mores. How many adults possessed that much courage?

If he'd pigged out on the heart-shaped sugar cookies she'd brought to the daycare party, she'd be worried about his intake of sweets. But after one bite of the one she'd given him, he'd handed it back. Like her, chocolate was more his speed.

When she walked with him into the living room, Garrett was crouched next to the fire shifting the logs around. Georgie spared him a quick glance before continuing to the kitchen nook. She went with him, because he wasn't tall enough to put the tray on the counter.

He handed it to her and opened the dishwasher. After she rinsed everything, he loaded it on the racks.

"Good job."

"Yep." He glanced at her. "Grit maked the fire."

"Right." Technically she had, but she'd gladly share credit if it meant Georgie considered it a worthwhile contribution.

"I maked a Val-tine." He pointed to it with obvious pride.

"You did! And I love it." She walked to the fridge and crouched down so they were both eye-level with the big red heart he'd stuck on the door with Spiderman magnets.

Inside the heart, two wobbly black circles each contained dots that might be eyes and a curvy line that might be a mouth. A family portrait. She put her arm around his shoulders. "I'll keep it forever."

He nodded. "I know."

"Let's go make s'mores." She gave him a squeeze and stood.

"Grit gots boots."

Interesting comment. "That's right." Evidently he didn't mind Garrett having boots. Maybe he even liked it. The Babes could be onto something.

By the time they returned to the living room, the coals glowed invitingly and Garrett had laid out all the supplies. He sat on the right side of the couch, leaving plenty of room on the left for her and Georgie.

With a hand on his small shoulder, she guided him around the left end and picked up a toasting fork. Sticking a marshmallow on the end, she turned to hand it over. But he wasn't beside her.

Instead he'd marched down to Garrett's end of the couch. He stood in front of him, back straight. "I gots boots."

She pressed a hand to her mouth to hold back a startled laugh.

"Nice boots." Garrett's voice sounded strained, as if he might be having trouble keeping a straight face, too.

And that was it. Georgie walked back to her. She handed him the fork and they started making s'mores. So did Garrett.

Nobody talked. She was afraid to say anything and upset whatever strange détente was going on. Garrett kept his silence, too. Every so often Georgie would look at Garrett, but he never ventured back there.

After they'd all made several s'mores, Garrett stood and carried his fork into the kitchen nook. The sound of running water indicated he was washing off the fork.

Georgie used his stage whisper. "*What's he doin', Mama?*"

"I think he's getting ready to leave."

"Oh."

Was that disappointment in his voice? Sounded like it.

Garrett came out of the kitchen nook and walked to the front door. "Thanks for the s'mores." He plucked his coat off the rack and shoved his arms into the sleeves. "Have a good—"

"Wait." Getting to her feet, she walked to the door. "We didn't decide—" She stopped herself before she said something incriminating.

Garrett pitched his voice low. "Six." He put on his hat.

"Got it." She gazed at him and mouthed the word *progress.*

He smiled and gave a short nod. Then he touched two fingers to the brim of his hat and went out the door.

When she turned, Georgie was staring at the closed door. "Grit goed home."

"Yes. Want to make one more s'more before you go to bed?"

"Yep." But clearly he missed their silent, boots-wearing guest.

Well, join the club. So did she.

# 26

His A-game. Yeah, right. D-game was more like it. Garrett swore softly as he turned off the engine of his washed and detailed truck.

He should have it together by this point in his life. Instead he was more nervous than a green teenager picking up his first date. Loading this night with expectations was a recipe for disaster and he'd done it, anyway.

He wanted the next twelve hours to be like a slowly toasted marshmallow, a gentle build-up of passion that culminated in the sweetest, most tantalizing love-making either of them had ever experienced. Was that too much to ask? Yes, it was.

Opening the door, he checked the slushy ground near the running board. For sure he'd get his polished boots covered in muck walking up to the porch. He leaned over and opened the passenger door. Anna's footing would be just as bad. Her loafers would end up a mess.

Should've paid more attention to the landscape instead of obsessing about the evening ahead. Closing both doors, he backed out and drove in at a different angle so the passenger side was only a few feet from the bottom step.

Anna came out and waited on the porch as he was resituating his truck. Her white parka covered whatever top she'd worn, but she'd opted for a denim skirt instead of jeans. Red boots had replaced the loafers he was used to seeing.

He hit the button that lowered the passenger window. "I didn't like my original parking job."

"I was hoping you hadn't changed your mind about our date."

"Not a chance. Hang on and I'll come around to help you in."

"That's silly. I'll just—"

"Please let me." He opened his door.

She laughed. "Well, if it means that much to you."

"It means that much to me." He put the window up and climbed out. He'd be damned if he'd just swing by and expect her to hop in.

The footing wasn't bad, so his boots didn't take much punishment as he rounded the hood of the truck, grasped her hand and helped her into the passenger seat.

She glanced at him and smiled. "I think you spit-shined this truck."

"I think you're right. Are those new boots?"

"They sure are. When I was in the store with Georgie yesterday, I noticed they were having a half-price sale on red ones for Valentine's Day. Georgie and I went back today and I bought these."

"Snazzy." He closed the door, hurried around, and swung into the driver's seat. "Your first pair of boots?" He pulled the door shut, enclosing them in the warmth from the heater.

"I used to have some." She buckled up. "Before I met Brad, my girlfriends and I would go dancing at a country-western place in Indianapolis. Brad didn't dance, especially country, and I gave them away. But I like these even better. Can't wait to try 'em on the dance floor."

"And here I thought I'd be introducing you to something new."

"You are. I'm letting someone keep my kid overnight. I still can't believe I'm doing it. Henri's promised to call or text if she has any issues."

"He's in good hands." He put the truck in gear and headed out. They were off. And chatting like normal. Good start.

"It's like when I put him in daycare, except different. I've never left him overnight with anyone. I felt very weird driving away from Henri's, but as time goes by, I'm adjusting to it."

"Was Claire already there?"

"She was. The minute Georgie saw her, he was all in. Then Henri brought out her little stuffed moose named Ben to meet Carl. After the two furry friends got acquainted, she took us all down to the basement to show off Charley's trains."

"Charley had trains?"

"Sure did."

"That's news to me."

"Nobody's touched them since he died. She couldn't face those trains and the Brotherhood couldn't bear to go down there, either. She almost hired someone to dismantle everything and find a buyer, but she couldn't bring herself to do that, either. It's a gorgeous layout."

"Georgie must be over the moon. I would have been at his age."

"He was delirious when he saw them. Claire was dazzled, too. I confess I was fascinated, myself. I mean, who didn't have a train set that ran around the Christmas tree at some point in their childhood?"

"I didn't."

"Did you like trains?"

"Loved 'em. Wasn't in the cards for me to own any though. I could buy a train set now, but what would be the point? I have nowhere to put it."

"You don't need to buy one. Just go ask Henri if you can mess around with Charley's. I think dusting them off for the kids and getting them running again did her heart good."

"Probably."

"If Henri's okay with the trains, now, maybe the Buckskin gang could have fun with them again."

"I'll bet they would." He hesitated. "This might not work out, but trains might be something else Georgie and I could agree on. Besides boots."

"Wasn't that amazing when he made a point of showing you his? I think you had to be part of his decision to get some. Ed didn't put any pressure on him to go this route."

He grinned. "I don't think it's wise to force anything on Georgie."

"You picked up on that, huh? By the way, he was sad when you left last night."

"You think so?"

"Definitely. We made a couple of s'mores afterward, one for each of us, but his heart wasn't in it. He loved going back to shop for my boots today, though. He walked up and down the aisles, pointing out boots that looked like yours."

"How do you know he was thinking about me?"

"Oh, I don't know. It might have been the way he pointed at each pair and said either *Grit* or *nope, not Grit.*"

"Wow. That does feel like progress."

"That's not all. Tonight, when I left Henri's and told him goodbye, he touched two fingers to the brim of his hat."

"Where'd he learn that?"

"You did it last night as you were leaving."

"I suppose I did. It's an automatic thing with me."

"Well, he noticed and he copied you."

"I'll be damned."

"For the record, I noticed, too. That's the kind of move that gets my heart thumping."

"Oh, yeah?"

"It's polite, subtle and sexy. I don't like seeing you leave, but you sure look good doing it."

He glanced at her. "You always look good. I like your hair like that." She'd worn it down and added some waves. He couldn't wait to get his hands in it. Taking a quick breath, he returned his attention to the road.

"That's nice of you to say. I've been so kid-focused since Georgie was born that I haven't spent much time on myself. I got out the curling iron tonight for the first time in months." She ran her fingers through the dark, glossy strands.

The motion sent a sweet fragrance his way. Her shampoo, most likely. He'd be treated to that scent while they danced at the Moose. Later he'd be surrounded by it when they... uh-oh. His body liked that prospect a little too much. And they were only a few minutes into the evening.

She'd stopped talking. Was it just him, or had the temperature in the cab gone up several degrees? Her breathing had changed, too.

She shifted in her seat. "All I brought tonight was my phone and my key."

"That's..." He paused to clear the huskiness from his throat. "That's all you should need." Should he mention what he'd brought?

"I noticed there's a duffle in the back seat."

"It's a change of clothes." And condoms. "In case I need to head straight to the barn. I have barn duty in the morning."

"I promise not to make you late."

He met her gaze. The air sizzled and he broke eye contact immediately. Driving off the road wouldn't add to their evening's enjoyment. "I know you wouldn't. It's me I'm worried about."

"Are you prone to oversleeping?" She sounded amused.

"No, ma'am."

"Well, I might. For almost three years I've had a kid who needs attention first thing in the morning. What a luxury not to have that responsibility." The teasing note was still in her voice.

"Then I'll be careful not to disturb you."

"What if I want to be disturbed?"

His jeans began to pinch. "Then I'll be at your service."

She groaned. "You win. I thought I could play this sexy game without it getting out of control."

"Is it out of control?"

"Almost. I have half-a-mind to ask you to turn the truck around."

"I have half-a-mind to do it."

"But the gang is expecting us."

"Yes, they are, and you've never been there for one of our outings. We should go, have a nice meal and dance a few times."

"I want that, too. I've been practicing my shimmy."

"Practicing your... shimmy?" Yeah, he was toast.

"Kate and Millie taught Isabel and me how the other night."

"Of course they did." Way to throw gasoline on the flames, ladies.

# 27

Anna had been in the Choosy Moose a couple of times with Brad before Georgie was born. She'd laughed at the large plush moose head mounted over the bar and tapped her foot to the music from the country band.

Tonight, bright red hearts dangled from the moose's antlers and she was here with a crowd eager to hit the dance floor. She couldn't wait to experience the Moose the way it was meant to be enjoyed.

The Buckskin gang commandeered two adjoining horseshoe-shaped booths. Soon after the servers returned to the kitchen with everyone's order, the band launched into Kip Moore's *Somethin' Bout a Truck*. The booths emptied out with cries of *the truck song*.

Garrett led Anna to the dance floor and called over to CJ and Isabel. "Bet you requested this."

"You know it. If Izzy and I only get a couple of dances, this had to be one of them." CJ twirled Isabel onto the floor.

"It's a gang favorite." Garrett pulled her into his arms. "CJ plays it for us on fire pit nights. Ready?"

"Sure am." Giddy with anticipation, Anna matched her movements to his as they circled the floor in a fast two-step. Not long into the dance, he put her through some tricky maneuvers. "If this is a test, bring it on, cowboy."

"Dancing with you is a test, all right. Testing the heck out of my self-control."

"Is that so?"

"Yes, ma'am. That tight red top…"

"I wore it to go with the boots." She hadn't dressed provocatively in forever. Hadn't wanted to.

"Nice try. You wore it to drive me crazy."

She smiled. "Does it?"

"Take a guess. I'm adding more complicated moves to distract myself from… other things."

"I see." Now she had her mind on other things, too. She bungled a step and accidentally nudged his arm with her breast.

He tightened his hold. "Playing dirty, are we?"

"That was your fault. I missed a step because you brought up… the other thing."

"I'm doing my level best to keep it down."

She flashed him a grin. "I'm sure it's very hard."

He spun her in a double twirl and hauled her up against him. "I'll let you be the judge."

The music ended, but he didn't let go. Like the rest of the Brotherhood, he'd left his hat on for the dancing. Hats added to the manly visual and the challenge of dancing while wearing it. These guys clearly relished both.

The Stetson's brim shadowed Garrett's eyes, but there was no mistaking the glow of passion in their blue depths. Or the heat coming from his aroused body.

The band switched to a slow tune, and he began to move, keeping their hips aligned, his gaze locked with hers and his hands clasped behind her back. "You turn me inside out, Anna."

"Ditto, Garrett." She rested her palms on his chest and matched her breathing to his.

"After this song, the food should be coming out."

"Can't wait." She breathed in the scent of his aftershave as his heartbeat vibrated against her palm.

"I couldn't care less about the meal." He massaged the small of her back. "But once we eat it, we're that much closer to leaving."

His low, intimate tone stoked the fire racing through her veins and she shivered. "I know I objected to the eat and run plan before, but—"

"Tell you what. Let's at least stay for the traditional line dance with the gang. CJ and Isabel need to leave early, so odds are somebody will ask the band for a line dance tune once everyone's finished eating."

"Then we can go?"

"Then we can go."

A line dance. The perfect opportunity to show off her shimmy.

* * *

Garrett's prediction was right on target. As plates around the table grew empty, the band announced a line dance she'd learned in Indianapolis, the Cowboy Cha-Cha. She caught Millie's eye and smiled. Millie gave her a quick thumbs-up. Kate and Isabel exchanged a glance. Game on.

She turned to Garrett. "I know this one."

"Then let's get out there." Taking her hand, he led her to the dance floor.

They lined up beside CJ and Isabel with Jake and Millie in the row ahead of them. Millie turned to give her a wink.

Garrett tapped Millie on the shoulder. "What are all the signals about, lady? You up to something?"

"I'm always up to something."

Jake laughed. "I'll vouch for that."

The band played the intro to Shania Twain's *I'm Gonna Getcha Good!* and Millie threw her hands in the air, let out a whoop and started them off.

Anna had to concentrate for the first few bars, but once she'd grooved in the pattern, she loosened up enough to deploy her first shimmy. The first one was tentative and Garrett wasn't watching, anyway. Kate, Millie and Isabel were shimmying their hearts out. Time to go for it.

The next time, Garrett got an eyeful. His jaw dropped and he made the wrong turn on his next step. She started to giggle. Garrett wasn't the only stumbling cowboy out there. CJ, Rafe and Jake had a determined clench to their jaws. Their shimmying women were clearly playing havoc with their dancing prowess.

Damn, this was *fun*. Anna threw herself into the movement with reckless abandon, swept away by the music and the lyrics. She ended the dance out of breath and grinning.

Her three friends converged on her as they all exchanged high-fives. Millie yelled out *shimmy power* before Jake grabbed her around the waist and hustled her off the floor.

"We'll do this again, soon." Kate gave her a hug and strolled over to link her arm through Rafe's. Isabel left with CJ, alternately waving and doing fist pumps.

"That was something."

She turned and gazed into Garrett's eyes. "It was supposed to be."

"I just about swallowed my tongue."

She smiled, her heart still beating fast. He had the bluest eyes in the world, especially when they flashed with fire, like now. "That was the idea."

"Ready to leave?"

She swallowed. "Yes."

He held up their coats and her purse. "I took a chance you would be. Let's go."

## <u>28</u>

Garrett figured he and Anna must have talked about something on the way back to her cabin. But he had no clue what had been said. She'd fried his brain with that shimmy routine.

One dance had told him who she was when she allowed the burden of her responsibilities to slip from her slender shoulders. That sensual woman had captured his heart, a heart that ached for all she'd suffered in the selfish grip of a bastard, a heart that yearned to make up for it a hundred times over.

He pulled in as close to the steps as he dared and switched off the engine. "Let me get you out."

"That would be lovely."

Her soft voice flowed over him like warm honey.

"In fact, can I have your key?"

She dug in her little purse and handed it over without question.

Climbing out, he grabbed his duffle and his hat from the back seat. "Be right back." Closing the door, he rounded the front of the truck, took the steps two at a time and crossed the porch in three strides. He let himself in and carried his duffle back to her bedroom.

She'd set the scene—low light, covers turned back. He left his coat on a chair over by the dresser, took the condoms out of the duffle and laid them on the bedside table. Once she was in his arms, he wouldn't want to let go.

Hurrying back outside, he left the door open, clattered down the steps and opened the passenger door.

She glanced at him. "Aren't you freezing?"

"No, ma'am." When she started to get down, he scooped her into his arms. "Let's do it this way."

"Garrett, I can—"

"I know." He nudged the door shut. "I want to."

Her voice gentled. "Okay." She wrapped her arms around his neck as he carried her up the steps. "This is unnecessary, but very romantic."

"That's what I'm going for." Once they cleared the door, he gave it a shove with his boot and it swung closed with a muted click. He started down the hall.

"Just so you know, you don't have to woo me. I'll give you anything and everything you want."

His groin tightened as he stepped into her bedroom and slowly lowered her to her feet. "How about you let me do the giving?"

She gazed up at him and her breath hitched. "I don't... I don't know what that looks like."

Her hesitant confession stole the last piece of his heart. "I'll show you."

After divesting her of her coat, he had her sit on the bed so he could take off her boots.

"You'll laugh when you see what's underneath. I wore them in case we needed some comic relief."

He tugged off both boots at once and grinned. "Spiderman socks."

"Got them when I bought Georgie's last summer. He was so excited when they had them in my size, too."

"They look great on you." He slowly peeled them off. Laying them aside, he crouched in front of her, took one foot in both hands and began a slow massage.

"Thanks."

"Not as great as your red top, though." Lowering her foot to the carpet, he lifted the other one, massaging with a firm touch, his attention on the pace of her breathing as it slowly picked up speed.

"I've had it a while. Left it in the closet, waiting for the right time. This was it."

"I'm glad I was there." He slid his hands up her calf and his massage shifted to a gentle caress.

"You were the reason I wore it."

"I'm honored." Easing up the hem of her skirt, he rested his hands on her knees. "I'll never forget watching you shimmy in that red top."

"I'll never forget it, either. I felt like Captain Marvel—flying through the air and giving off sparks."

"You sure set me on fire." Using gentle pressure, he urged her knees apart.

She sucked in a breath. "What are you doing?"

"Getting to the good stuff." He leaned in and placed a kiss on her inner thigh.

"Shouldn't we start taking off—"

"Not yet." The denim was stretchy, allowing him to push it up some more. He continued his leisurely journey, placing soft kisses first on one thigh, then moving over to the other. He breathed in the sweet scent of arousal. "I think you like this." He added a swipe of his tongue to the mix.

"You're giving me the shivers."

"That's only the beginning of the giving train." He pushed her skirt high enough that he could hook his thumbs into the waistband of her panties. "Lift up."

"I still think we should take off more clothes." But she did it.

"If we take off more clothes, I might forget to serve the appetizer." He pulled her panties off and left them next to her socks. "Let me know how you like it." Slipping his hands under her deliciously bare tush, he lowered his head and flicked his tongue over the sensitive rosebud begging for his attention.

She gasped and sank back onto the bed.

"Good?" He repeated the move.

"Very..." She gulped as he did it one more time. "Very good."

"All I need to know." He tasted, nibbled and licked until the woman who'd shimmied to that

Shania Twain song emerged, crying out for more, her body throbbing with promise.

She came in a glorious rush of moist pleasure. With her nectar on his tongue, he rose to his feet, leaned down, and gave her a deep, sensual kiss that nearly made him come, too.

Grasping his head, she sucked on his tongue while he fought the climax that demanded to join with hers. If he hadn't left his clothes on... but he'd meant to do that, meant to use that as a barrier to keep him from taking her the second they were alone in this bedroom.

Slow and easy. That was his intention. But a red haze of lust sabotaged his noble goal. Pulling her red top from the waistband of her skirt, he slid his hand underneath the soft knit and found—hallelujah—the front clasp of her bra. A flick of his wrist and it gave way.

He eagerly stroked the tempting breasts that had participated in a shimmy that would live forever in his fevered brain.

She broke away from the kiss. "I want you naked."

He laughed. "I want you naked."

"Then let's get to it, cowboy. Take off your clothes and I'll finish taking off mine."

"Deal." He pushed himself upright and made short work of the job. Boots got tossed aside, socks thrown somewhere, shirt left where it fell, jeans and briefs in a crumpled pile he stepped out of.

"Oh, wow." She stood by the bed, surveying him from head to toe.

He gave himself the same privilege. "Wow, yourself." He drank in the sight of creamy breasts blushing pink from his fondling and burgundy nipples taut with arousal. Her slim waist and curvy hips showcased the treasure he'd recently discovered between her satin thighs.

He craved her with a persistent ache that had begun the day they'd met and might never go away. She was the one. He'd never been so sure of anything in his life.

She came toward him, her dark eyes alight. "Make love to me, Garrett. I want to fly through the air and give off sparks."

He drew her into his arms. "If I can make that happen, I'll be the happiest man on Earth."

"My money's on you." She rubbed both hands over his pecs. "I was hoping you had chest hair. I like that."

"Why?"

"It makes us different."

He chuckled. "That's not the most obvious thing that makes us different."

"No, but every guy has one of these." She gripped his cock. "Although not every guy has one like yours."

His balls tightened, ready for action. "As I said, at your service."

"I'm liking this idea of being naked."

He leaned down and gave her a soft kiss, one completely at odds with the inferno raging inside him. But he'd hang onto his civilized side as long as possible. "Me, too." He walked her backward until they tumbled onto the bed.

What the move lacked in gracefulness it made up for in expediency. The moment they were horizontal, the fun began. She explored his body with a spirit of adventure, toying with his cock, plucking at his nipples, running her fingers through his chest hair.

He couldn't keep his hands off her, either. Her breasts provided an endless source of pleasure, but he loved touching every part of her he could reach, from her sleek backside to the hollow of her throat, to the erotic zone between her thighs.

During one of his adventures there, as he'd stroked a finger into her cleft, she'd uttered a low, throaty groan. "It's time."

Way past time for him, but he wasn't opposed to playing around until she was ready. "Yes, ma'am." Swinging his feet to the floor, he stood and made use of the condoms he'd left on the bedside table.

As he rolled it on, he gazed at her lying on the bed, watching him. Had any woman ever looked that beautiful? He had his doubts. "Do you have a favorite?"

"Favorite what?"

"Position."

"I do, and if that makes me boring, I apologize in advance."

He laughed. "You could never be boring. Missionary, right?"

"Right."

He climbed onto the bed and moved between her thighs. "My favorite, too."

"Wait." She grasped his face in both hands. "I didn't mean to put pressure on you by saying I wanted to fly and give off sparks."

He smiled. "It's not pressure. It's a challenge."

"But if that doesn't happen, it's okay."

Balanced on one hand, he stroked her moist channel. She was wet and ready. He eased forward. She hadn't figured it out yet, but they were a dynamite combination. Flying and giving off sparks was a no brainer. He smiled. "It'll happen."

# 29

Anna held her breath as Garrett pushed gently inside. Fooling around was one thing, but would they match up when... oh, yes, they most certainly would. Perfect fit. Epic, in fact. She'd never... oh, dear God, he felt *amazing*.

"Well?"

She gazed up at him. "This works."

He grinned. "Not going to make me pack up and go home?"

"No." She cupped his firm buns. "Stay. Please."

"Can I move a little? I don't have to, but usually it makes for a nicer—"

"Moving would be good."

"Glad to hear it." He began a subtle rocking motion.

"This way we can see..." She gasped as the gentle friction put her senses on high alert.

"How're you doing, Anna?"

She dug her fingers into his glutes. "I feel like I'm—"

"Flying and giving off sparks?" He bore down and increased the pace.

"Oh, Garrett, this is... I've never..."

"Should I keep going?"

"Yes!" She clung to him, rising to meet each thrust, her body singing with joy as the delicious tension built deep in her core.

His breathing grew ragged as he pumped faster. "That's it, Anna. Shimmy for me."

With a wild cry, she let go, arching into the climax as her world exploded into a shower of sparks and sent her flying, flying...

With a deep groan, Garrett pushed in once more, burying his cock as far as it would go as he shuddered in her arms. She held him close, gasping for breath, wrapped in wonder.

\* \* \*

Garrett nuzzled the tender spot behind her ear. "Can't speak for you, but I was giving off sparks."

"Me, too." She ran her hands up and down his back, relishing the tactile pleasure of firm muscles under her fingertips. Strength was baked into this man. "Best ever."

He stilled. Slowly he raised his head and gazed into her eyes. "You mean that?"

"Yes." The words had slipped out, surprising her. But they were true. "What just happened feels...right."

"Sure does." The glow in his eyes intensified. "Best ever."

She stared at him. "What are we talking about?"

"I think we're talking about something... that might last."

Significant words. Her chest tightened. "Or maybe we had a great time at the Moose and that spilled over onto—"

"No." He sucked in a breath. "There's something going on here, Anna. Something important."

She reached up and stroked his cheek. "I swore I wouldn't get involved with anyone until Georgie was much older."

"I know."

"But I'm involved with you. You're always on my mind, and I—"

"Same here. Always thinking of you." Leaning down, he feathered a kiss over her mouth. "Always wanting you."

"You have me now."

"And I'm not wasting a single second of this night. Stay right here while I take care of the condom. When I come back, we'll talk."

"I'm too blissed out to go anywhere."

"I love hearing that." He kissed her again and climbed out of bed.

"Do you know where the bathroom is?"

He laughed. "It's a relatively small house. I can figure it out." He left the room. Seconds later his voice drifted from the hallway. "Nope. Closet."

"Far end!" she called out, laughing. He might not know where everything was located, but he filled a void in this cabin, one she hadn't admitted was there until now.

She could manage as a single mom. Plenty of women had done fine with it. And the wrong man was worse than no man. But Garrett wasn't the wrong man. He was the guy she'd dreamed of all her life. When she'd given up on finding him, she'd settled for Brad.

Complications still existed. Just because Georgie liked Garrett's boots and mimicked his two-fingers-to-the-hat gesture didn't mean he was ready to accept him as a part of their lives. But he might, someday.

Garrett walked back into the bedroom with an ease he hadn't had in this cabin until now.

"I feel like we just passed a milestone."

"Because we made love?"

"Well, that, but more because we both agree this isn't just a casual fling."

"I knew it wouldn't be. Not with the considerate way you've treated Georgie. Or the way—" Her phone pinged, signaling a text. She bolted out of bed. "Where's my phone? I don't remember—"

"Here." He pulled her small purse out of the pocket of her coat.

"God, I hope everything's okay." Her hand shook as she extracted the phone and tapped the screen.

*Just letting you know Georgie and Claire are fast asleep. All is well. Have fun.*

The breath whooshed out of her lungs. "Henri wanted me to know everything's fine."

"That was nice of her."

"It was, but she gave me a heart attack."

"I get that. Logically, though, she'd call if she had a big problem. We could easily miss a text."

She glanced at him. "You're right. If she'd texted while we were—"

"Exactly."

"I'm putting the phone by the bed. Just in case." She laid it beside the condoms. So many condoms. She started to laugh. "I see you came prepared."

"Better to have too many than not enough."

"I'd agree with that." She climbed back into bed and propped a pillow behind her back. Then she patted the spot next to her. "You were ready for a chat."

His gaze roamed the length of her, lingering on her breasts and her thighs before returning to her face. "I thought I was."

Her breath hitched as desire flared, bringing a hot flush to her skin. "We could postpone that discussion."

"Yes, we could." He approached the bed.

Her womb clenched in response to his aroused body. The proud jut of his cock promised another shattering release, a renewal of their magical connection.

They could talk later. Sliding down and turning on her side, she held out her hand. "Make love to me, Garrett."

# *30*

Panting and satisfied beyond his wildest dreams, Garrett lay on his back and held hands with Anna, who was breathing just as hard as he was.

The covers lay on the floor at the end of the bed. The room was cool, just the right temperature for wild lovemaking. No better way to work up a sweat than their recent activity.

He gave her hand a squeeze. "You okay?"

"Never better."

"Me, either. Cold yet?"

She chuckled. "Not yet. Want me to grab the covers?"

"No, I'll do it." He released her hand. "Have to get up, anyway." He swung his legs over the bed. "I have an idea. How about a nice warm shower?"

"I'm too boneless to make it in there. You go ahead."

"Okay." He started to pull the covers up to keep her warm. Then he changed his mind and left them the way they were.

In the bathroom, he dispensed with the condom before turning on the water in the shower stall. He briefly considered the tub, instead, but the tiled stall appealed to him more. The curtain instead of a door gave easy access. When the water was nice and warm, he returned to the bedroom.

She glanced at him. "Why are you here when the water's running in the shower?"

"Will you go in if I carry you?"

"I see where this is leading." A gleam lit her dark eyes.

"Will you?"

"I've never been carried by a naked man. Could be fun."

"I promise it will be." Rounding the bed, he leaned down. "Put your arms around my neck." Once she did, he slid both hands under her tush and picked her up. "Wind your legs around my hips."

"I like this already."

"Me, too. Sometime we should try it this way." Since he'd likely be back here on other nights when Henri offered to babysit, he looked forward to more opportunities to make love.

Carrying her into the steamy bathroom, he nudged the curtain aside and stepped in, her back to the spray.

She giggled. "Kinky."

"Never taken a shower with a guy before?"

"Never. You can put me down, now."

"Maybe I don't want to." He turned around and propped her back against the tile. "Maybe I'd rather do this." Leaning down, he licked drops of water from her breasts.

"Mm." She let go of his shoulders and cupped her breasts, lifting them up to his mouth.

"Nice." He tugged on one pert nipple with his teeth before taking it in and sucking as he squeezed her sweet behind.

He moved to her other breast, his cock rising as he indulged himself. Easing her feet to the tile, he kissed his way down her moist body and coaxed her thighs apart. On his knees, water pelting him, he revisited his favorite place, nibbling, licking and fondling her until... the best sound in the world echoed off the shower walls.

Holding her steady, he slowly stood and dropped damp kisses on her mouth and cheeks. "Like your shower so far?"

She gulped for air. "It's had its moments."

"Glad to hear it." He nuzzled the hollow of her neck. He would never get enough of this woman.

"Now it's my turn." Her sultry voice telegraphed her intention a second before she took a firm grasp on the situation.

He gasped as the urge to come nearly undid him. "Easy. I'm close."

"Then this won't take long, will it?" She maintained her hold as she got to her knees.

When her lips closed over the tip of his cock, he gasped again. Where was the self-control he'd honed over the years? Gone, replaced with a hair-trigger response.

He tried to last. He really did. Hands braced against the tile, he gave in embarrassingly soon. He might have yelled. Probably had.

Rising to her feet, she came up between his braced arms and kissed him. He cupped the back of her head, sliding his hand over her water-slicked hair, and kissed her back. "Happy Valentine's Day."

"Is it past midnight?"

"Yes, ma'am. Will you be my Valentine?"

"I will if you'll be mine."

"Love to." He kept kissing her until the water turned cold.

As he twisted the handles to shut it off, a jaunty tune drifted down the hallway.

"Uh-oh." Nudging him aside, she pushed the curtain open and raced naked down the hall. The tune stopped.

He grabbed a towel and hurried after her. "What—"

"It's Georgie." She tossed her phone aside and hurried to the dresser. "Earache. He's spiking a fever, screaming and crying, wanting me. They're bringing him over."

"Now?"

"I'm afraid so. Henri's driving as slow as she can. Do you think you can vamoose before they get here?"

"I'll do my best." He searched the floor for the clothes he'd flung off earlier. Henri's house was a very short drive away.

"I'm so sorry. I should have anticipated—"

"How could you?"

"It's winter. Kids get earaches this time of year." She wrenched open a drawer, grabbed underwear and pulled on a pair of panties.

Locating his briefs and jeans, he quickly tugged them on. "But he was okay when you left him, right?"

"Yep. Doesn't guarantee anything. Earaches can come on fast and often at night." She pulled a shirt off a hanger, making the others clack and jangle. "I didn't even think of it. Should have."

Popping the shirt over her head, she pushed her arms into the sleeves.

"It's bad luck, that's all." He grabbed his shirt from the floor, put it on but didn't button it. Leaned against the wall and yanked on his boots. "Everything could have gone smoothly. You couldn't know—"

"Jeans. I need jeans." She took the lid off a laundry hamper and jerked out a pair.

He put on his jacket and hoisted his duffle. "I'm outta here."

"Thanks. Again, so sorry." She stepped into one leg and hopped around trying to get the other leg in.

"It's okay." He'd almost made it to the front door when a truck pulled up outside. He turned back. "Anna, they're here."

She appeared in her bedroom doorway, her expression anxious.

He gazed at her. "What should I do?"

"Come back in here."

He started toward her as the rumble of the truck's engine ceased. "But won't he see my truck?"

"Maybe he'll be okay with it. Maybe—"

"Don't want Grit!" Georgie's frantic scream pierced the silence. "Don't want Grit! Nooooo! Want Mama! Nooooo!"

Anna rushed toward the door, her face drained of color as the screams continued, growing louder and more hysterical by the second. "Go into my room." Her breath came in gasps. "Stay there until I get him into his room."

His gut clenched. "Right." He lengthened his stride and ducked into her bedroom just as she flung open the door and raced outside without a coat. He stood in the middle of the room, breathing hard, those panicked screams tearing him to bits.

Georgie drowned out most everything else, except murmured words here and there. He identified Henri, Red and Claire. Yeah, he'd just stay here. He resisted the urge to put his hands over his ears.

Eventually Georgie's protests became less strident and were punctuated by sobbing. Had Anna taken him into his bedroom? Couldn't tell for sure.

Then Henri poked her head in. "Coast is clear."

"Thanks." Carrying his duffle, he followed her into the living room where Red stood with Claire. Everyone wore coats, but judging from their mussed hair and the combo of boots pulled over pajama pants, they'd all come directly from their warm beds. "I'm so sorry, ladies."

"We're sorry, too," Henri said. "I'm going to stay and see if I can help Anna. If you'll drop Red at my house and take Claire home, I'd be very appreciative."

"Let's go." He gestured toward the door and followed them out, grabbing his hat off the coat tree as he went by. He managed to reach the truck in time to open both the front and back passenger doors. "Claire, if you'd please go in the back."

"Gotcha, Uncle Garrett. Want me to take your duffle?"

"Thank you." He helped her in and handed it to her.

"Oh, wait. Mine's in Gramma Henri's truck."

"I'll get it in a sec." He handed Red up to the passenger seat, trotted around to the driver's side and climbed in so he could start the engine and turn on the heater. "Should warm up in a minute. Be right back."

When he returned with Claire's duffle, the murmur of voices from inside the truck stopped. He opened the back door and gave it to her.

"Thank you, Uncle Garrett." Her tone was soft, the kind she might use when talking to an invalid.

He got behind the wheel and put the truck in gear. "I appreciate what you all tried to do tonight. You did your best."

"It was just tough luck." Red sighed. "On Thursday night I debated offering you some of my crystals. They helped Rafe and Kate last fall. Now I wish I had given you some."

"Me, too," Claire said. "I never knew about those until you started talking about them tonight. I want to get some. Uncle Garrett, you should look into the crystal thing."

"At this point I'd rub cow patties on my face if I thought it would help."

"Eeuuww! Blech! Please don't do that."

"I'm kidding, sweetheart." He drove up next to Henri's walk and left the engine running. "Stay put, please, Red. I'll walk you to the door."

"I know you will, dear boy. I had no intention of jumping the gun."

After exiting the truck, he went around, helped her down and escorted her to the porch.

She gave him a hug. "Don't give up hope."

"Did you hear him? He was terrified."

"But he was sick and in pain. Keep that in mind."

"I'll try." He gave her a kiss on the cheek. "Goodnight."

By the time he returned to the truck, Claire had claimed the front seat. She glanced over at him. "I didn't think you'd mind if I switched."

"Glad to have you." He put the truck in gear.

"I don't understand. I thought Georgie was doing better."

"I thought so, too."

"But did you have a good time, at least? I mean, until this happened."

"Yes. I had a very good time." Best ever.

"Don't give up."

"Oh, I won't. But... there's no getting around it. We're back to square one." Or worse, but he wouldn't say that to his optimistic young friend.

"Daddy will be up when we get there."

"He will?"

"Henri texted him to say you'd be bringing me home because Georgie got an earache. She didn't want him to be startled."

"Good thought. Did you have a good time? Before the earache thing?"

"I had a *great* time. I can't wait to take Daddy to see those trains. Have you seen them?"

"Not yet. But I expect I will, soon."

"That's what Gramma Henri said. The Buckskin gang will have a train party one of these nights."

"Sounds terrific." He parked in front of the bunkhouse. "Time to get you to bed."

"Guess so. It's been quite a night."

"Uh-huh." No kidding.

Zeke met them at the door and hustled Claire off to bed.

Garrett hung up his coat and hat, left his duffle on his bunk and wandered into the kitchen. He should go to bed, too, but he doubted that he could sleep. After getting himself a glass of water, he leaned against the counter.

A moment later Zeke came in. "This sucks for you and Anna. But at least you had some time alone together before it all went to hell."

"We did. Wish I didn't have this feeling of impending doom, though."

"Claire said he was screaming really loud."

"He was. I'm afraid he thought I'd turned into the bad guy who was trying to separate him from his mother. That's what his dad used to do."

"Yeah, well, kids aren't at their best when they don't feel good."

"You're right. But—" His phone pinged with a text. "Excuse me a sec. That's her."

*Georgie's finally asleep and Henri's gone home. You may be asleep, too. I hope so. I'm really sorry. It was just too much too fast. I need to give Georgie time, specifically all of my time, after this meltdown. I don't know for how long. I want to help him overcome his fear, but for now, we need to take a break.*

Garrett handed the phone to Zeke so he could read it.

He scanned the text and swore.

"My thoughts, exactly." He met Zeke's sympathetic gaze. "You know the worst part?"

"You're in love with her?"

He swallowed. "Yeah. And that hurts like hell."

# 31

After two days of hell, Georgie's ear infection was gone. Although Anna wasn't in the habit of letting him sleep in her bed, she made an exception during their ordeal.

Jake insisted she take Tuesday off so she could get some sleep. She kept Georgie home from daycare and they slept the day away, ate some dinner and went to bed early.

The next morning, she returned to her normal routine, dropped Georgie at daycare and walked into the visitor center with a determined smile. Jake stood behind the desk, scrolling through messages on his phone. "Hey, Jake."

He glanced up and returned her smile. "Hey, Anna." His voice was subdued, though, not a typical mode for him. "How are you?"

"Better, now that Georgie's recovered."

"It's gotta be hell when your kid's sick."

"It's awful, especially when there's not a whole lot you can do except wait it out, knowing they're in pain. I put warm drops in his ears, gave him something to reduce the fever, but mostly I had to let his immune system do the work. Which it did, eventually."

"Sounds exhausting."

"It was. Thank you again for giving me another day off. I'll be happy to make it up whenever you—"

"Not necessary. Happy to do it. Does he get earaches often?"

"No, thank goodness."

"Rotten timing, though."

She took a breath. "Not really." She held his gaze. "It was a not-so-gentle reminder of where my priorities lie."

He frowned and opened his mouth. Closed it again and sighed. "Right."

"So what's happened since I've been gone? Did Millie get you the snow blower for Valentine's Day?"

"She did." His expression lightened. "Also some chocolate body paint from Racy Lace."

"Excellent."

"Uh-huh." His grin was more typical Jake.

Good. She didn't want awkwardness between them. "How about the hawk? How's she doing?"

"Almost ready to release her."

"That's awesome."

"Yes, ma'am." He picked up his hat from the desk. "I love it when we can fix 'em and send them back to the life they deserve." He glanced past her to the parking lot. "We've got visitors and I have paperwork waiting. Glad Georgie's better." Touching two fingers to the brim of his hat, he headed down the hall to his office.

She walked behind the desk and prepared to greet the elderly couple coming through the door. Jake likely had been ready to challenge her statement about priorities. Good thing he hadn't. She was hanging on by a thread as it was. The last thing she wanted to do was argue with her boss.

\* \* \*

As the days dragged by, the pain of cutting off contact with Garrett didn't go away, but it became bearable. Mostly. Except when she took a shower. Or made s'mores with Georgie. Or heard Shania Twain on the radio.

She'd worried about running into him accidentally, but that didn't happen. It was as if they lived miles from each other. Her job at the visitor center and his as a wrangler didn't create opportunities to meet. If her brakes hadn't gone out, they might still be relative strangers.

Millie was as friendly as ever, and if she had opinions about the situation with Garrett, she kept them to herself. She gave Anna the date for the next Brotherhood sleepover, which would be coordinated with another girls' night at Kate's house.

Henri invited her to bring Georgie down to the barn again and he loved it even more the second time around. Henri made no reference to the night of the babysitting disaster other than to say she was happy Georgie was better.

When Georgie asked about Claire, Anna got Zeke's number from Jake and arranged for Zeke to drop his daughter off for dinner and s'mores. Since Garrett wasn't there, Georgie and Claire played Candyland in the living room and ate at the table. Georgie made s'mores minus his Spiderman suit.

Claire didn't mention Garrett, either. That had to be intentional, as if she'd been given instructions not to. After all, she lived with the guy and mentioning him would have been a natural thing to do. Evidently the Buckskin gang had agreed not to interfere with Anna's decision. Clearly she'd made the right one.

After Claire left, Georgie helped her put the dishes in the dishwasher and clean the toasting forks. She crouched down to give him a hug. "Did you have a nice time with Sissy?"

He nodded. Then he put his hands on her cheeks, his way of making sure he had her attention. "Where's Grit, Mama?"

She almost fell over. "He's... I imagine he's at the bunkhouse."

"Why didn't he comed here with Sissy? She wouldn't tell me."

Her chest tightened. "I didn't invite him."

"Why?"

"Because he upsets you."

"No, he doesn't."

Her breath hitched. "He doesn't?"

Georgie pressed his hands to her cheeks and stared into her eyes. "He's nice. He maked the fire. He maked 'mores. He liked my boots."

Her heart pounded. "Georgie..." She cleared her throat. "Do you miss Garrett?"

He nodded. "He's nice, Mama. He's quiet."

"Would you like me to invite him over?"

He nodded again.

"When?"

"Now, Mama."

* * *

Garrett had grown used to the constant ache of loss, but it was sharper tonight. Claire was over at Anna's place. Zeke had dropped her off, returned to the bunkhouse and suggested playing checkers.

Checkers was as good a distraction as anything, but he'd lost every game. At least it had passed the time until Zeke left to pick her up. They were due back any minute. He'd forced himself to sit by the wood stove like a normal person and pretend to be reading a book.

When they came through the door, he glanced up. "How'd it go?" Keeping his tone casual took effort, but he was determined to hold it together for Claire's sake. He laid his book aside.

She shrugged out of her coat. "Georgie misses you."

"He *what?*" Something must be wrong with his hearing.

"He misses you."

"He said that?"

"Not in so many words, but he asked me where you were. I told him you were in the bunkhouse. He wanted to talk about you, and I had to tell him I wasn't supposed to."

He groaned. "I didn't mean you couldn't talk to Georgie about me. That would have been fine." More than fine.

"Well, you didn't say that, so I was sticking to the rules."

"I appreciate that." Everybody had been great, including Claire. He'd requested zero interference and they'd all complied. "And you're right. I should have been more specific regarding Georgie."

"It's okay." She gazed at him with eyes that held more wisdom than any eight-year-old he'd ever met. "Anna's sad."

He sucked in a breath. "I'm sorry to hear that. But did you have a nice time?"

"We did, but it was... different."

"Different?"

"Georgie didn't wear his Spiderman suit. I love seeing him wear it with his hat. It's hysterical."

"But he only did that to hide from me."

"I guess, but I think he got a charge out of putting on a disguise. Tonight wasn't quite as... interesting."

Zeke smiled. "It's about to get even less interesting, sweetheart. Bedtime."

"Is it? Can I look at your phone, Uncle Garrett? I'll bet it's not nine yet."

He picked it up from the table and handed it to her. "Read it and weep."

"Oh, shoot, it's past nine! How did it get so late? I—" The phone pinged with a text and her eyes widened. "It's from Anna!"

His heart stalled. "Give it to me."

She handed it over. "You're supposed to say *please*."

"Sorry." He tapped the screen.

*Georgie has asked to see you before he goes to bed. He has something to show you. Could you possibly come over now? Please?*

He closed his eyes and ducked his head as he struggled to control a very unmanly reaction. *Breathe, dude. Just breathe.*

"Uncle Garrett?"

"He needs a moment, sweetheart."

Dragging in air, he lifted his head and handed the phone to Zeke.

"Oh, wow." He smiled. "That's more like it."

"Can I see, Daddy?"

"That's up to your Uncle—"

"She can see." Garrett stood, his legs a little shaky, his breathing still not up to par. "And I'm outta here."

"Go for it, man." Zeke clapped him on the shoulder. "Should we expect you back, do you think?"

"I don't know." He stared at Zeke. "I'll take this one second at a time."

"Wise move."

Claire hugged him around the waist. "Go get 'em, tiger."

He laughed. "Thanks, sweetie. I don't know what we ever did without you around here."

"I don't, either." She gave him a grin.

He carried her grin and Zeke's encouragement with him as he drove over to Anna's. He parked fast and made it to her door even faster.

She answered his knock, her eyes wide with surprise. "You're here! When you didn't text back, I thought—"

"I didn't?" He shoved his hand in his coat pocket. No phone. He'd left it with Zeke. "Guess I didn't. Sorry about that."

"It doesn't matter. Come in."

"You look beautiful."

Her smile trembled. "So do you."

He stepped inside. "You said Georgie—"

"I maded you a Val-tine." The little boy stood back, his hat pulled down, his expression cautious. He clutched a big red paper heart that looked exactly like the one from the fridge.

"You did?" Throat tight, he crouched down and thumbed back his hat.

Georgie approached slowly and held it out.

He took it carefully in both hands. It was the same one he'd seen on the fridge, two circles with dots for eyes and wavy smiles to represent Georgie and his mom. If Georgie wanted to pass it off as brand new, he'd take it and be grateful. "Thank you very much. It's a terrific Valentine."

"I know."

"Turn it over," Anna murmured.

He flipped the heart. The same two circles were on the other side, but underneath was a third, also with dots for eyes and a wavy smile. He swallowed. Blinked a couple of times.

At last he trusted himself to look up. Georgie had crouched down and pushed back his hat. His hopeful expression split Garrett's heart wide open. "Is this me?" He pointed to the third circle.

Georgie nodded. "I maded it."

"Wonderful job."

"Yep."

Now what? He held up the Valentine. "Should I take this with me?"

Georgie looked stricken. "You goed home?"

He sucked in a breath. "You don't want me to?"

"No. Stay here. In *my* house."

He glanced at Anna. Was this for real?

She made a little sniffling sound, but her gaze was steady. "You should stay in *our* house. If you want to."

They wanted him to stay. *Both* of them.

"I want to."

"Okay!" Georgie smiled.

He'd never seen Georgie smile. If the little boy hadn't already captured his heart, that smile would have clinched the deal.

Anna blew her nose. "It's Georgie's bedtime." Her voice was thick with emotion. "Make yourself at home. I won't be long."

"I'll be waiting."

Leaving his coat and hat on the coat tree, he sat on the couch and listened to the soft murmurs of Anna putting Georgie to bed.

The light in the bedroom flicked out. "Goodnight, Georgie."

"Grit's here, Mama."

"Yes, he is. Sweet dreams, son." She appeared and started toward him.

He rose to his feet. "I can't believe this is happening."

She came straight into his arms and tilted her tear-streaked face to his. "I can't, either." She wrapped her arms around him and held on tight. "I'm so sorry I gave up on us."

"Georgie didn't."

"Because you'd worked your way into his heart. Clearly he idolizes you."

He soaked up the emotion shining in her dark eyes. "How about his mama?"

"I don't idolize you."

"Guess I have more work to do, then." He leaned down. "More kissing, more—"

"I love you."

He stared at her.

"Are you surprised?"

His brain struggled to believe, but his heart was totally into it. "Yes, ma'am. You said you were *involved,* but that's not the same thing."

"It is the same thing. I just wouldn't admit it. How could I not love you? You're everything I've ever wanted. For me, and for my son. On top of that, *you* love *me.*"

"Figured that out, did you?"

She nodded.

"Ready to hear me say it?"

The glow in her eyes grew brighter. "Can't wait."

He framed her face with both hands and held her gaze. "I love you, Anna. I love your devotion to Georgie, your can-do spirit, your generous heart and your shimmy. I'm crazy about your shimmy."

"Was that the clincher?"

"No, the clincher came much earlier."

"When?"

"The first time I kissed you. And every time since then." He leaned closer. "Including this one." He touched his lips to hers, his heart filled with gratitude for this moment and the promise of all the ones that lay ahead.

\* \* \* \* \*

**Saddle up with cowboy Zeke Lassiter in
SINGLE-DAD COWBOY, book eight in the
Buckskin Brotherhood series!**

\* \* \* \* \*

*New York Times bestselling author Vicki Lewis Thompson's love affair with cowboys started with the Lone Ranger, continued through Maverick, and took a turn south of the border with Zorro. She views cowboys as the Western version of knights in shining armor, rugged men who value honor, honesty and hard work. Fortunately for her, she lives in the Arizona desert, where broad-shouldered, lean-hipped cowboys abound. Blessed with such an abundance of inspiration, she only hopes that she can do them justice.*

*For more information about this prolific author, visit her website and sign up for her newsletter. She loves connecting with readers.*

**VickiLewisThompson.com**